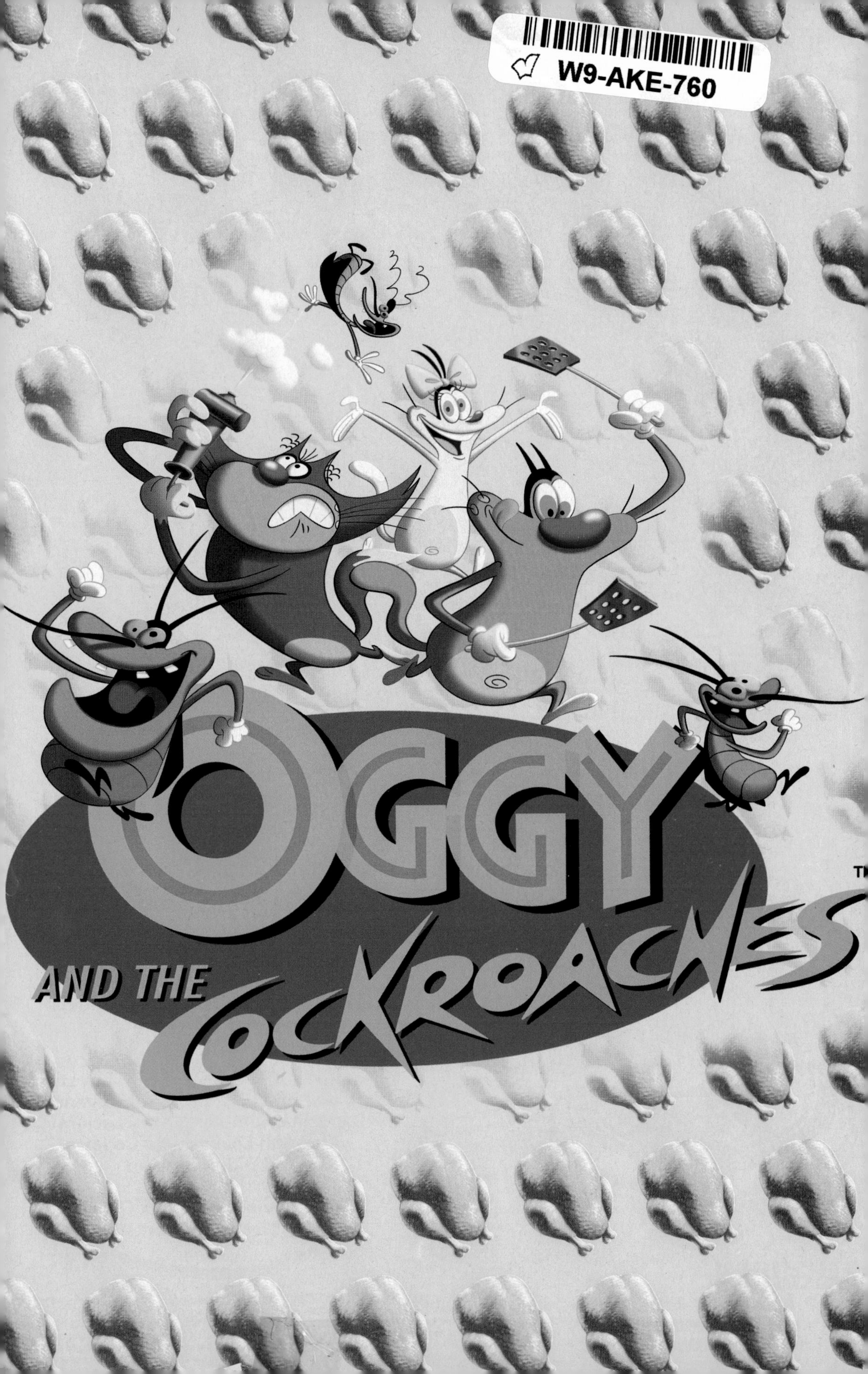
OGGY™
AND THE
COCKROACHES

Xilam

"A BUMP IN THE NIGHT"

Written by Jordan Gershowitz
Illustrated by Dean Rankine
Colors by Jeremy Kahn
Letters by Natalie Jane

"20,000 COCKROACHES UNDER THE SEA"

Written by S.A. Check
Illustrated by Dean Rankine
Colors by Jeremy Kahn
Letters by Natalie Jane

"RORRIM RORRIM"

Written by S.A. Check
Illustrated by Dean Rankine
Colors by Jeremy Kahn
Letters: Patrick Alan Wiseapple

"CULINARY CAT-ASTROPHE"

Written by Anthony Zicari
Illustrated by Dean Rankine
Colors by Jeremy Kahn
Letters by Natalie Jane

"TICK OR TREAT"

Written & Illustrated
by Dean Rankine
Colors by Jeremy Kahn
Letters by Natalie Jane

"UNHEALTHY COMPETITION"

Written by Jordan Gershowitz
Illustrated by Dean Rankine
Colors by Jeremy Kahn
Letters by Natalie Jane

Publisher – Michael Bornstein
President – James Kuhoric
Marketing Manager – Barlow Jones
Production & Design –
Patrick Alan Wiseapple

Extra Special Thanks to the Xilam staff –
Marc du Pontavice, Morgann Favennec,
Capucine Humblot, Cathy Leclere.
Kim-Anh Lê, Lorraine Collet,
and Didier Degand,
and to
Leslie Levine and Scott Cherrin
at Licensing Works!

AMERICAN MYTHOLOGY PRODUCTIONS

www.AMERICANMYTHOLOGY.net
Facebook: /AmericanMythologyComics
Twitter: @AmericanMytho

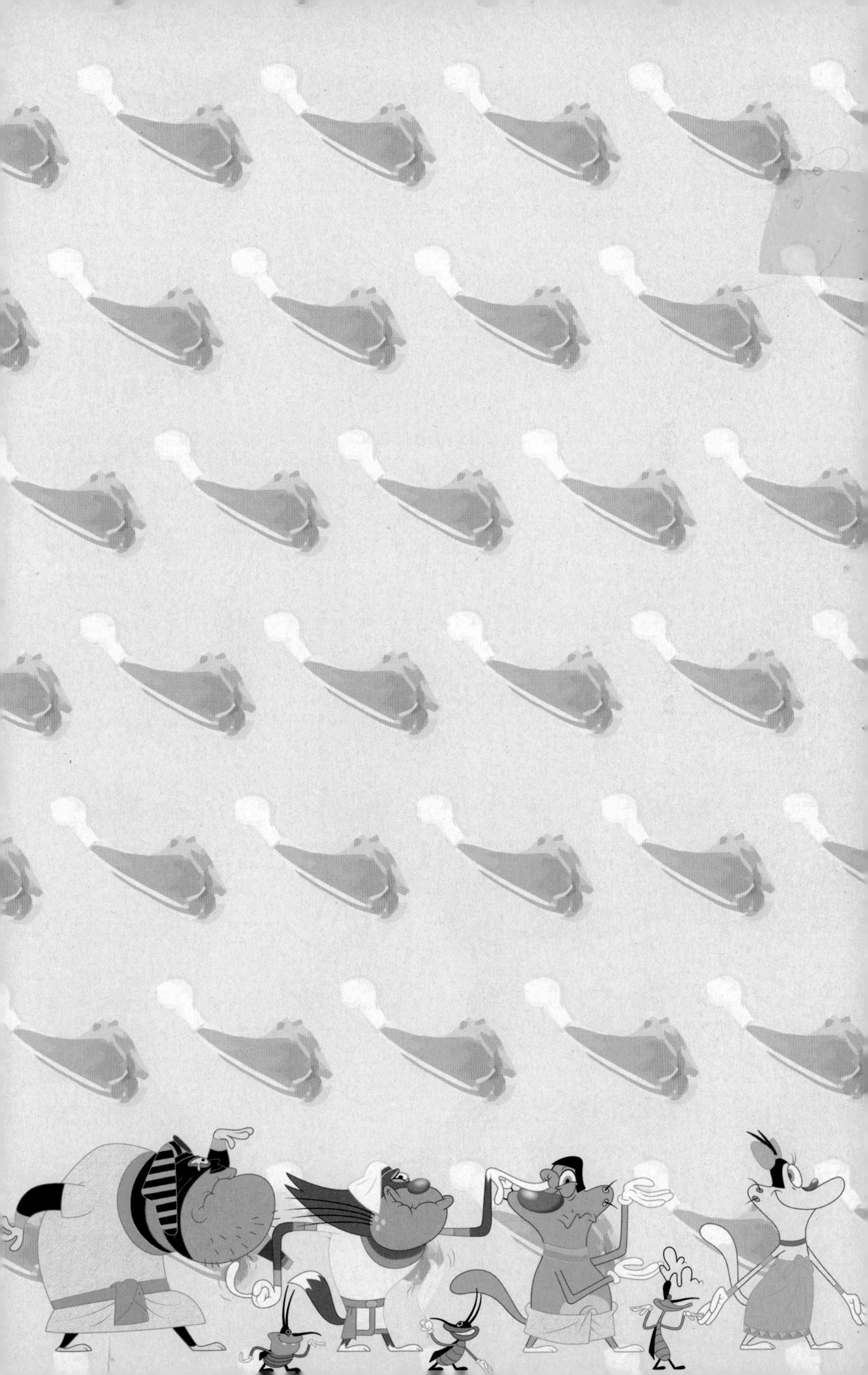

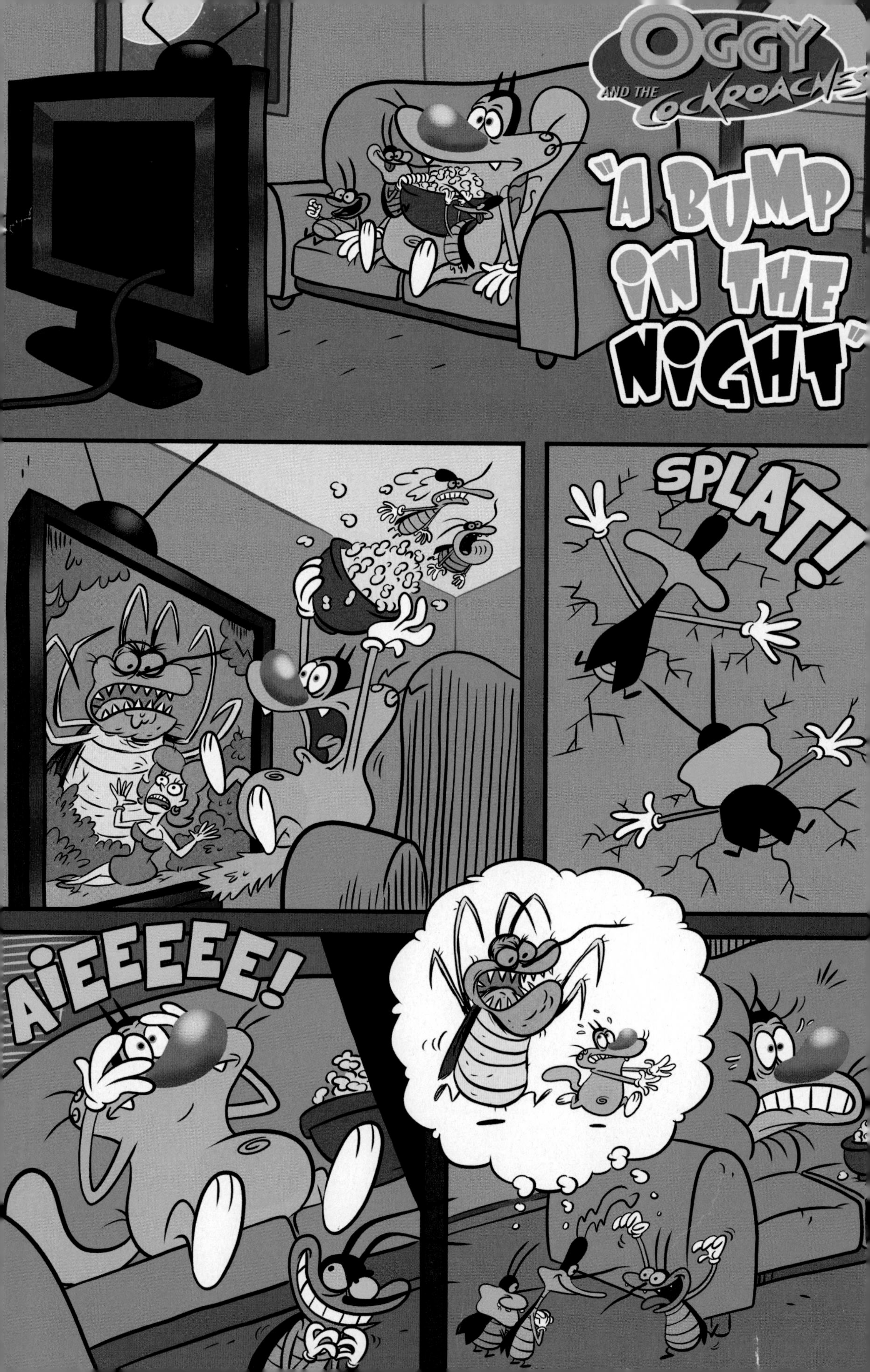
OGGY AND THE COCKROACHES
"A BUMP IN THE NIGHT"
SPLAT!
AiEEEEE!

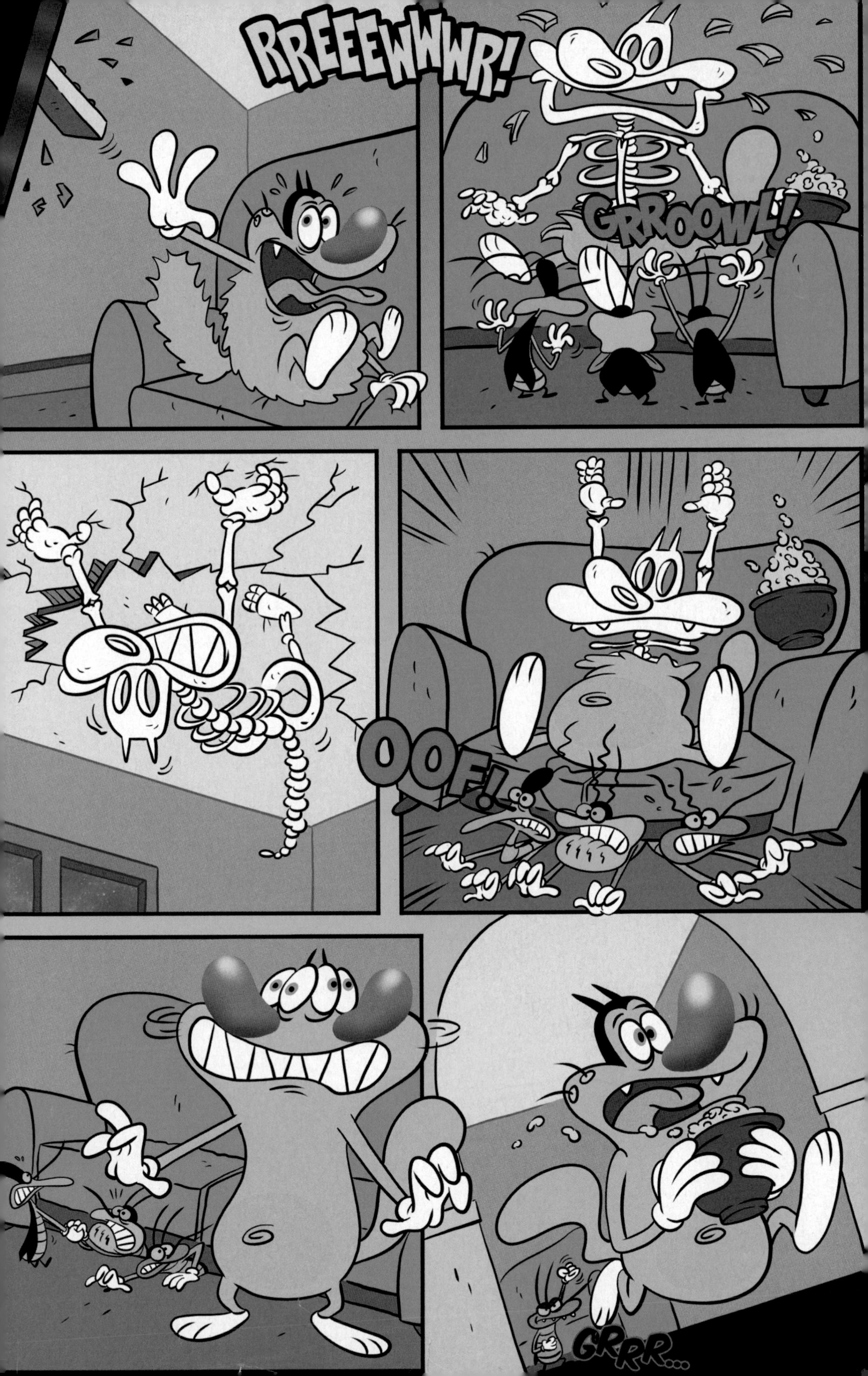
RREEEWWWR!
GRROOWL!
OOF!
GRRR...

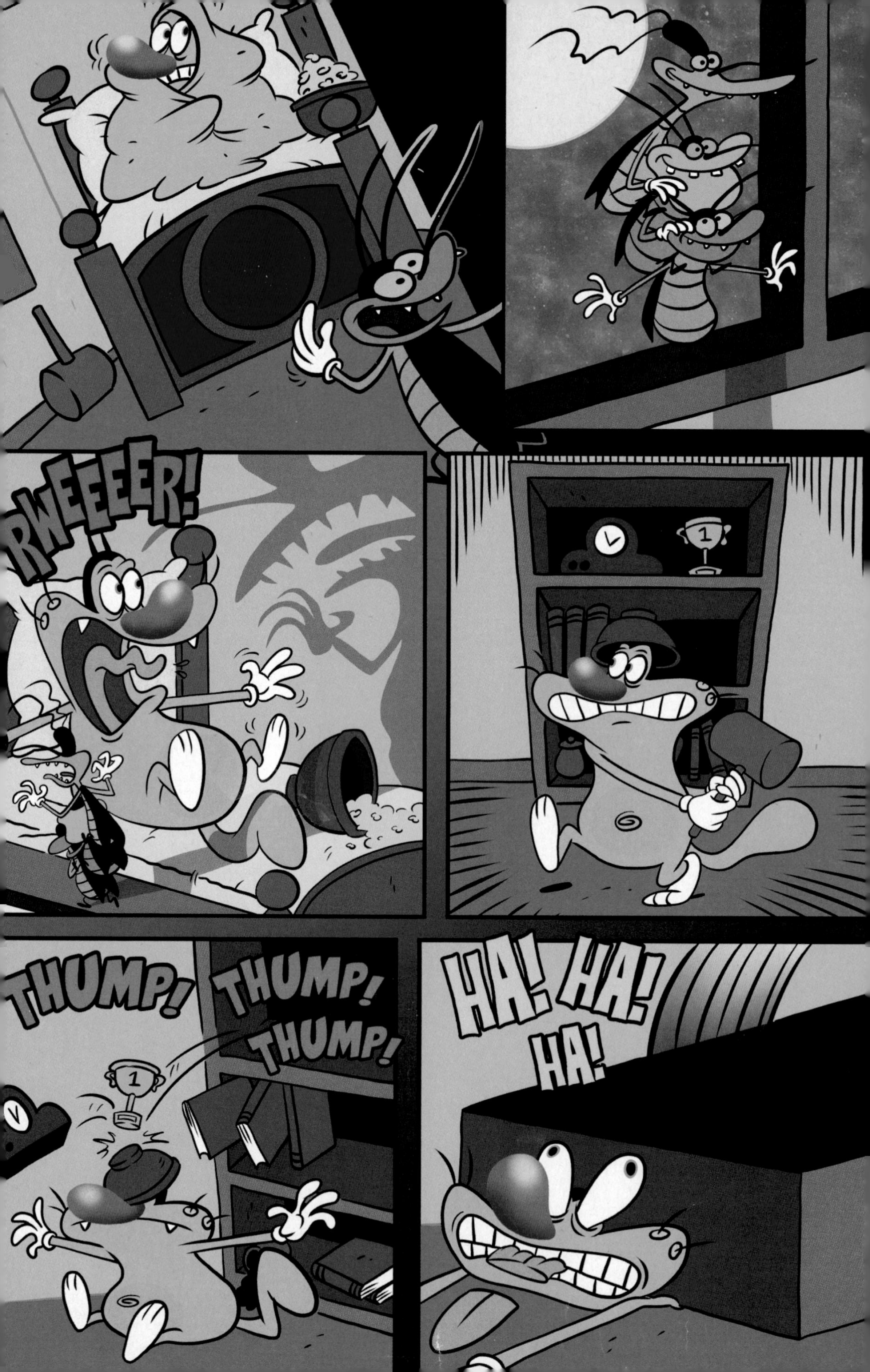
RWEEEER!
THUMP!
THUMP!
THUMP!
HA! HA!
HA!

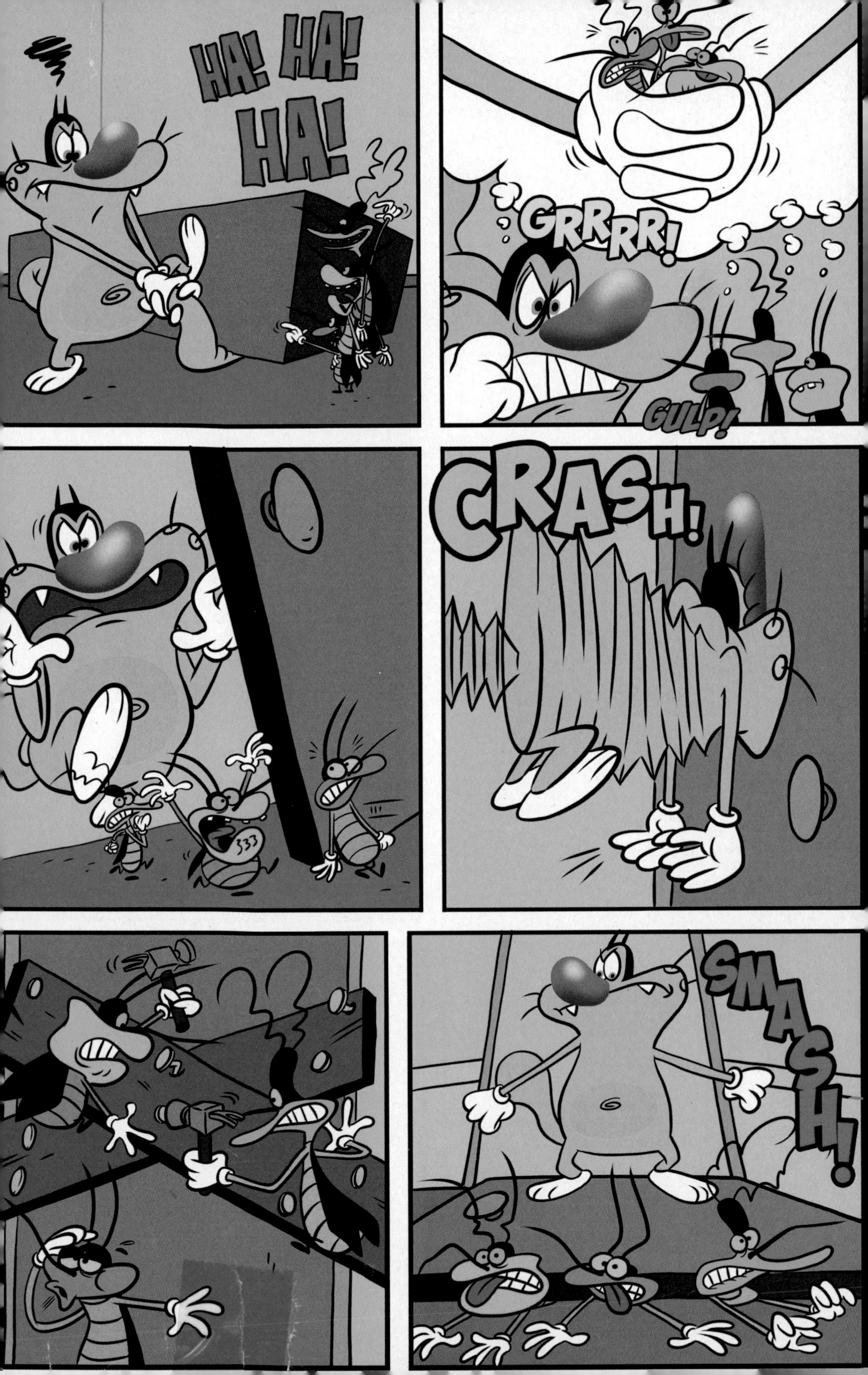
HA! HA!
HA!
GRRRR!
GULP!
CRASH!
SMASH!

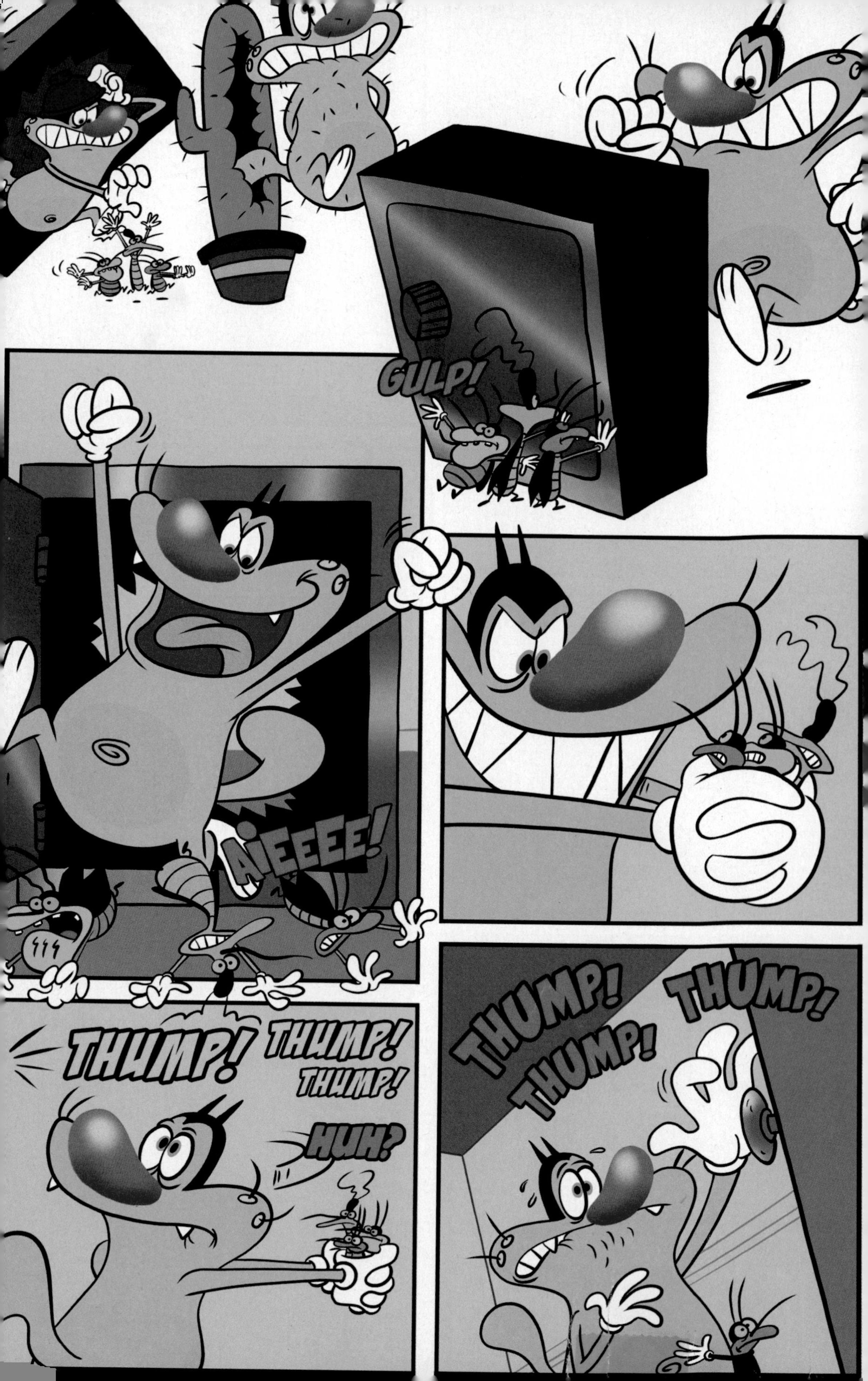
GULP!
AIEEEE!
THUMP!
THUMP!
THUMP!
HUH?
THUMP!
THUMP!
THUMP!

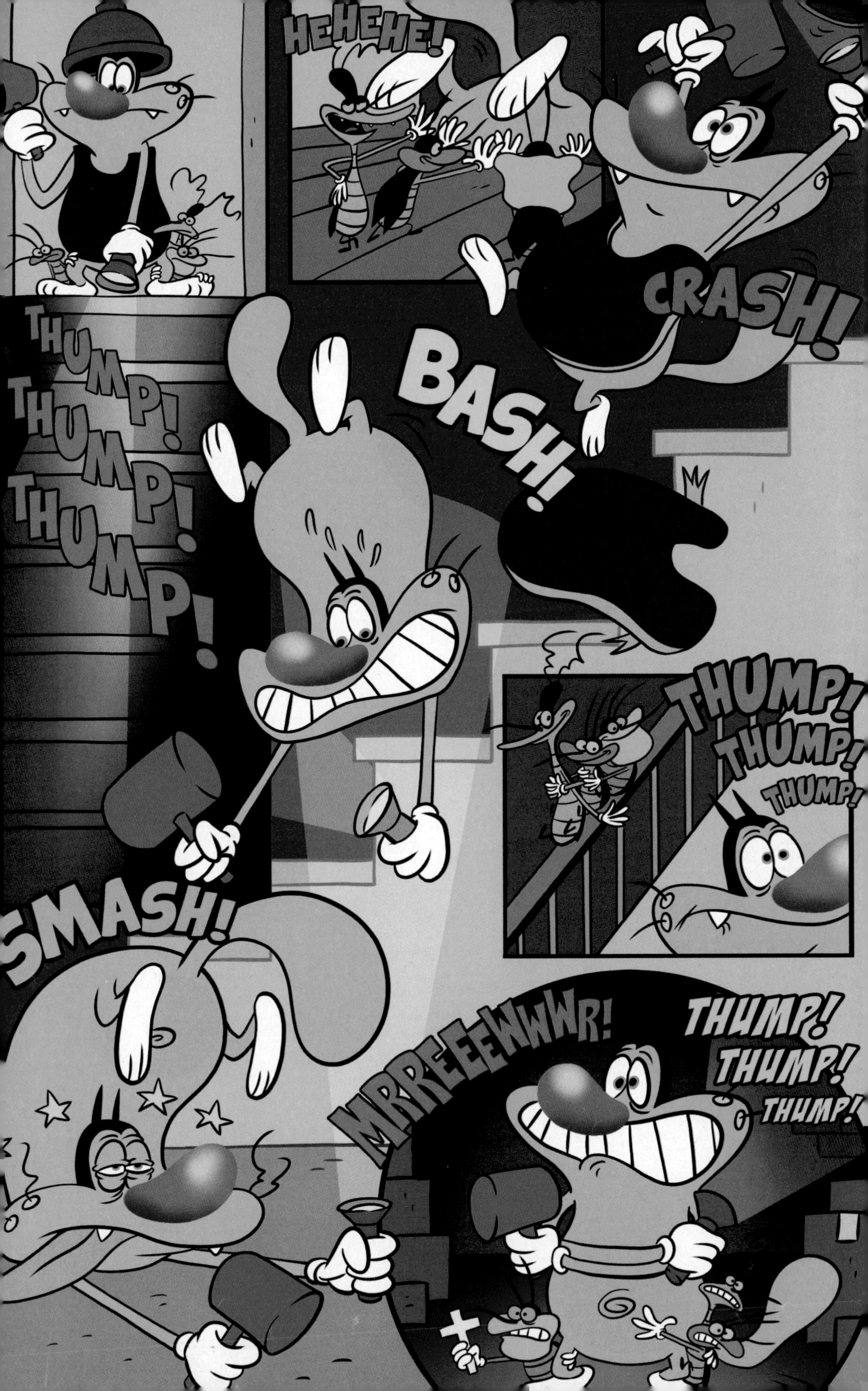
HEHEHE!
CRASH!
THUMP! THUMP! THUMP!
BASH!
THUMP! THUMP! THUMP!
SMASH!
MRREEEENWWR!
THUMP! THUMP! THUMP!

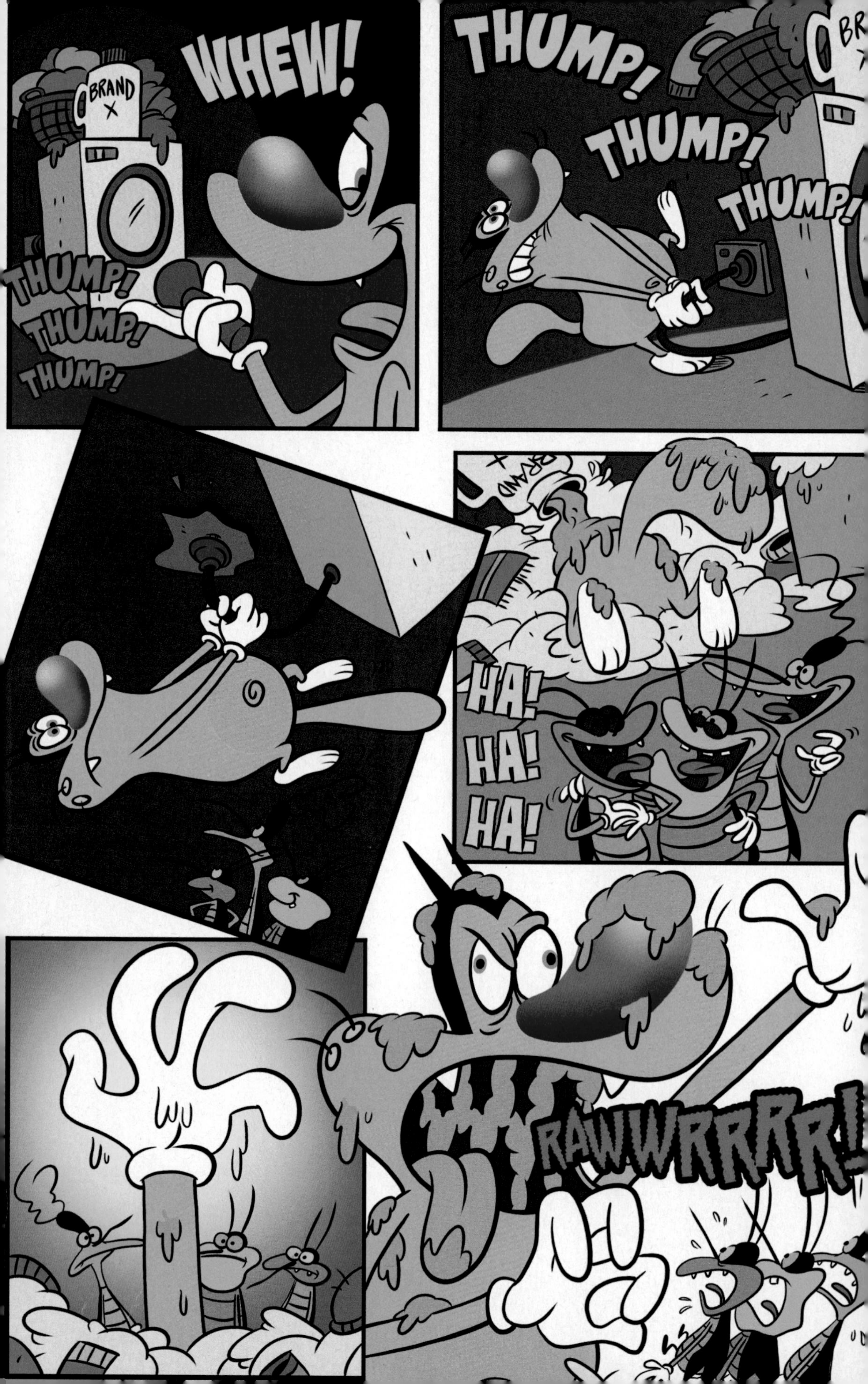
WHEW!
THUMP! THUMP! THUMP!
BRAND X
THUMP! THUMP! THUMP!
HA! HA! HA!
RAWWRRRR!

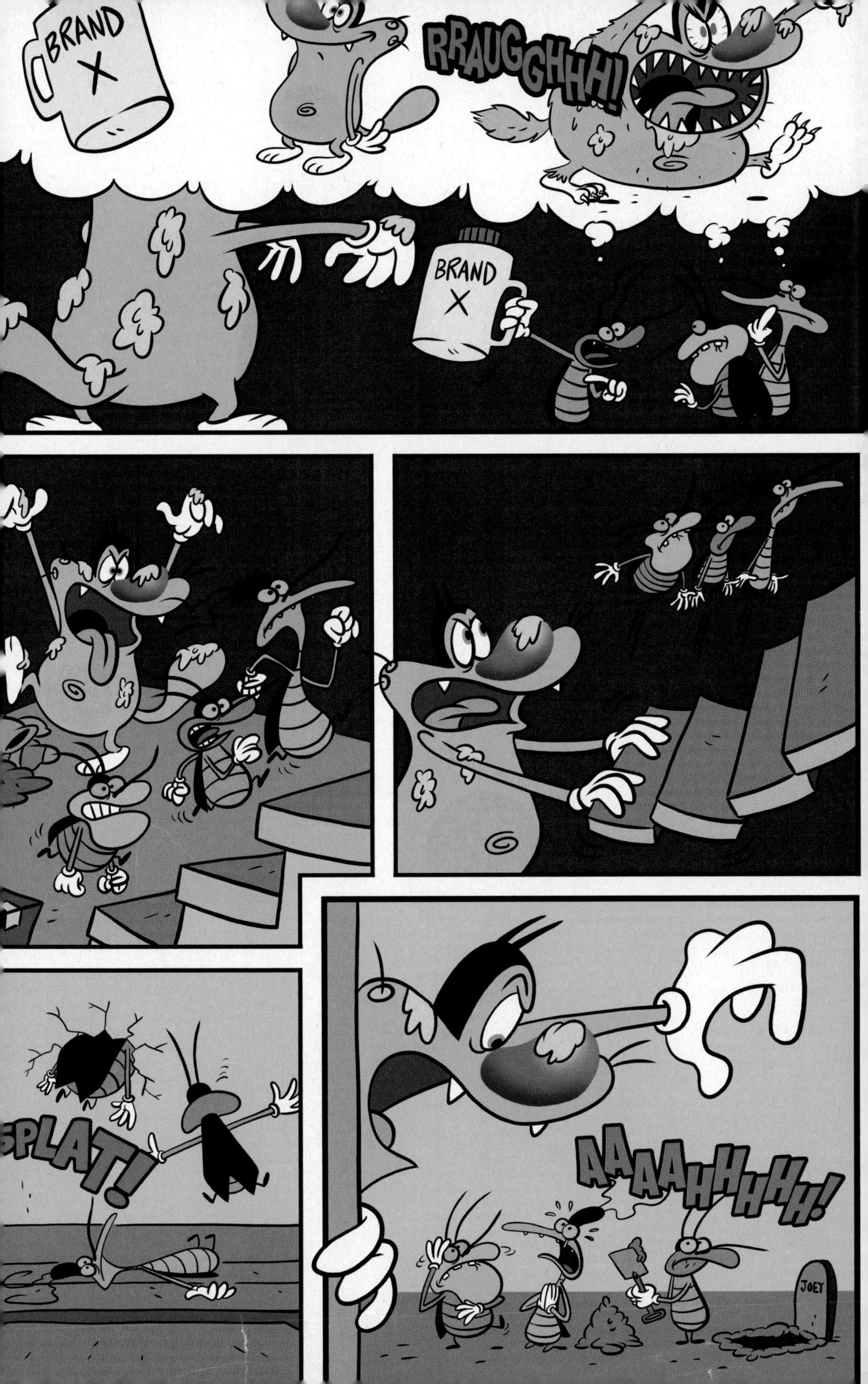
BRAND X
RRAUGGHHH!
BRAND X
SPLAT!
AAAAHHHHH!
JOEY

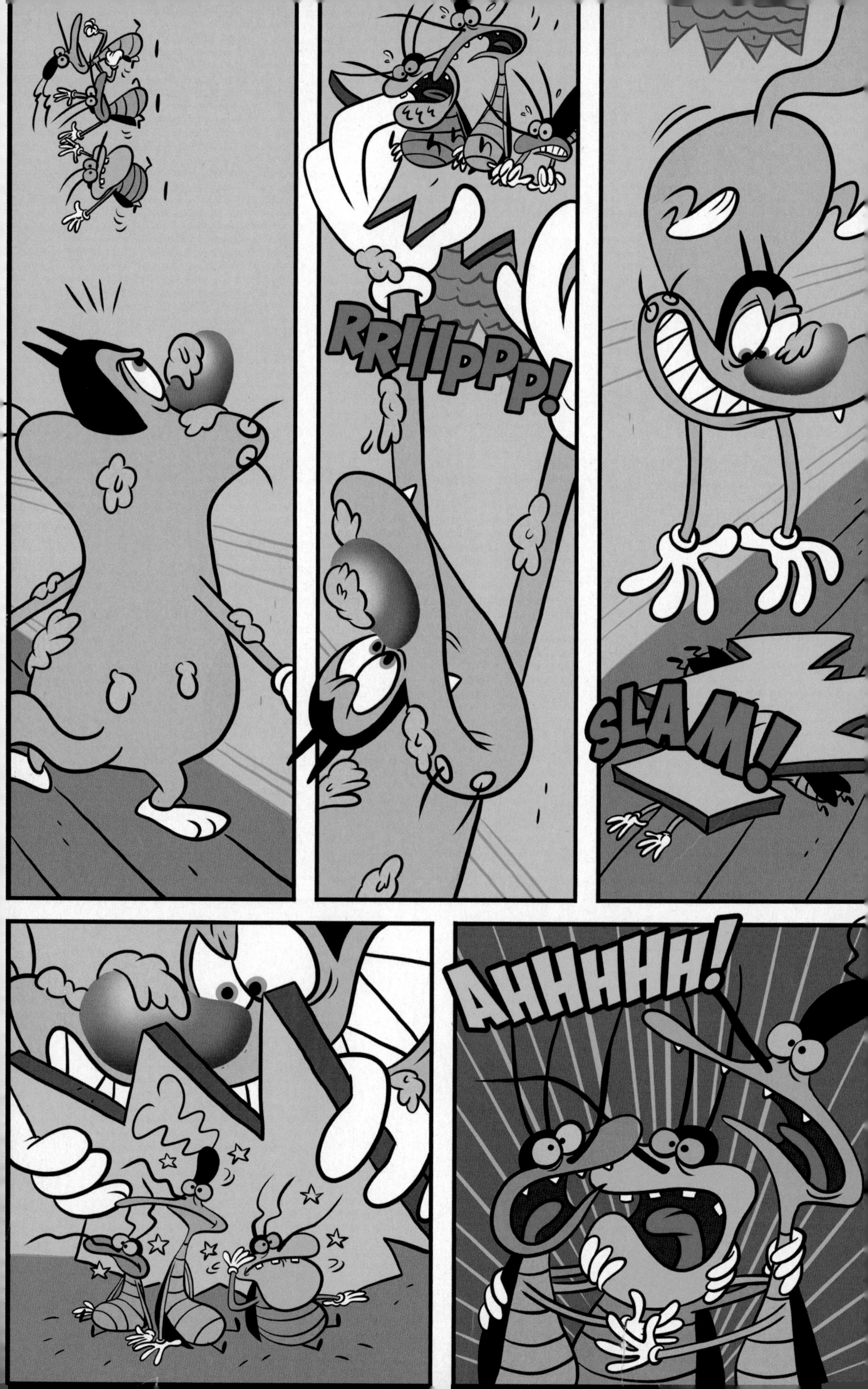
RRIIIPPPP!
SLAM!
AHHHHHH!

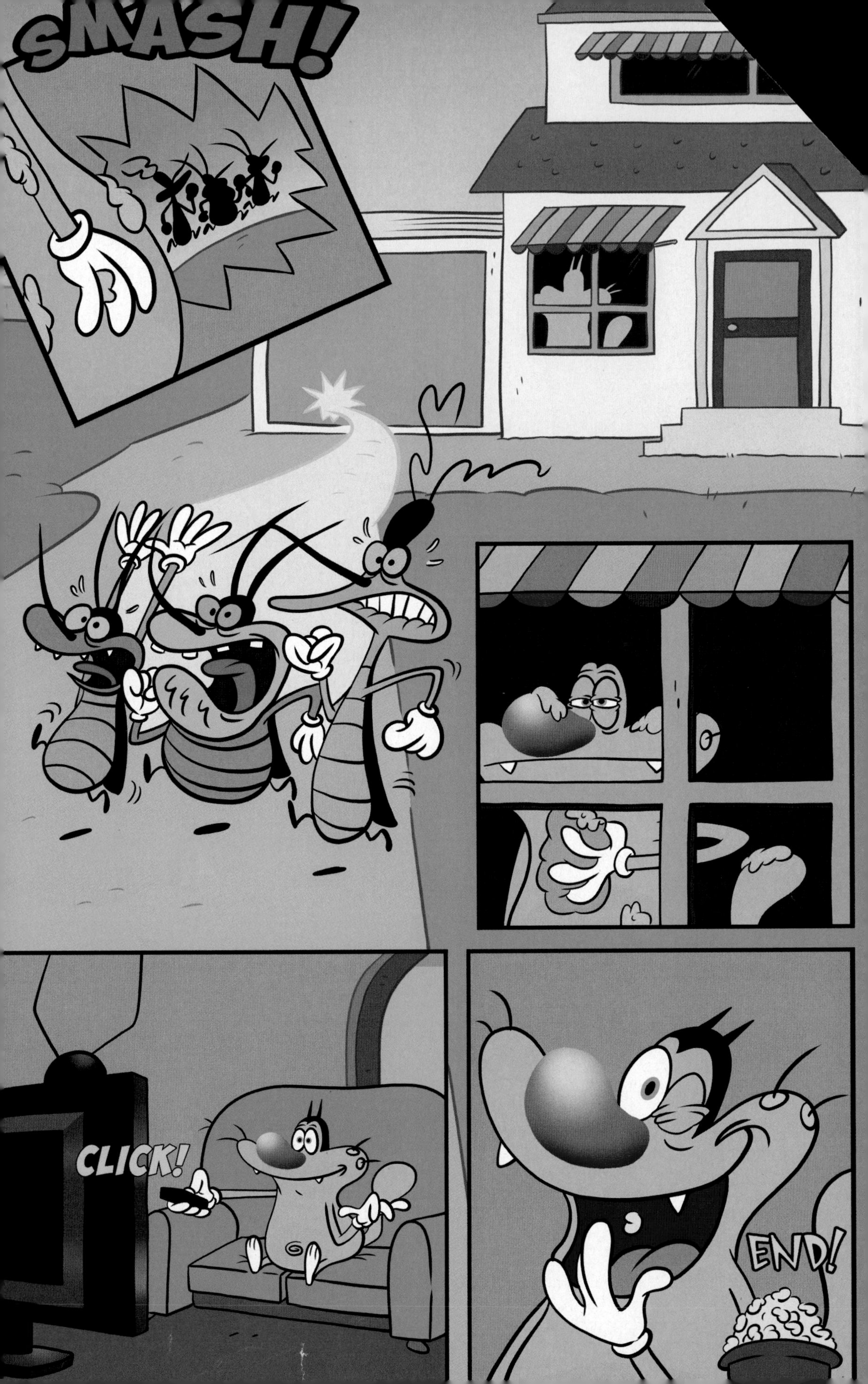
SMASH!
CLICK!
END!

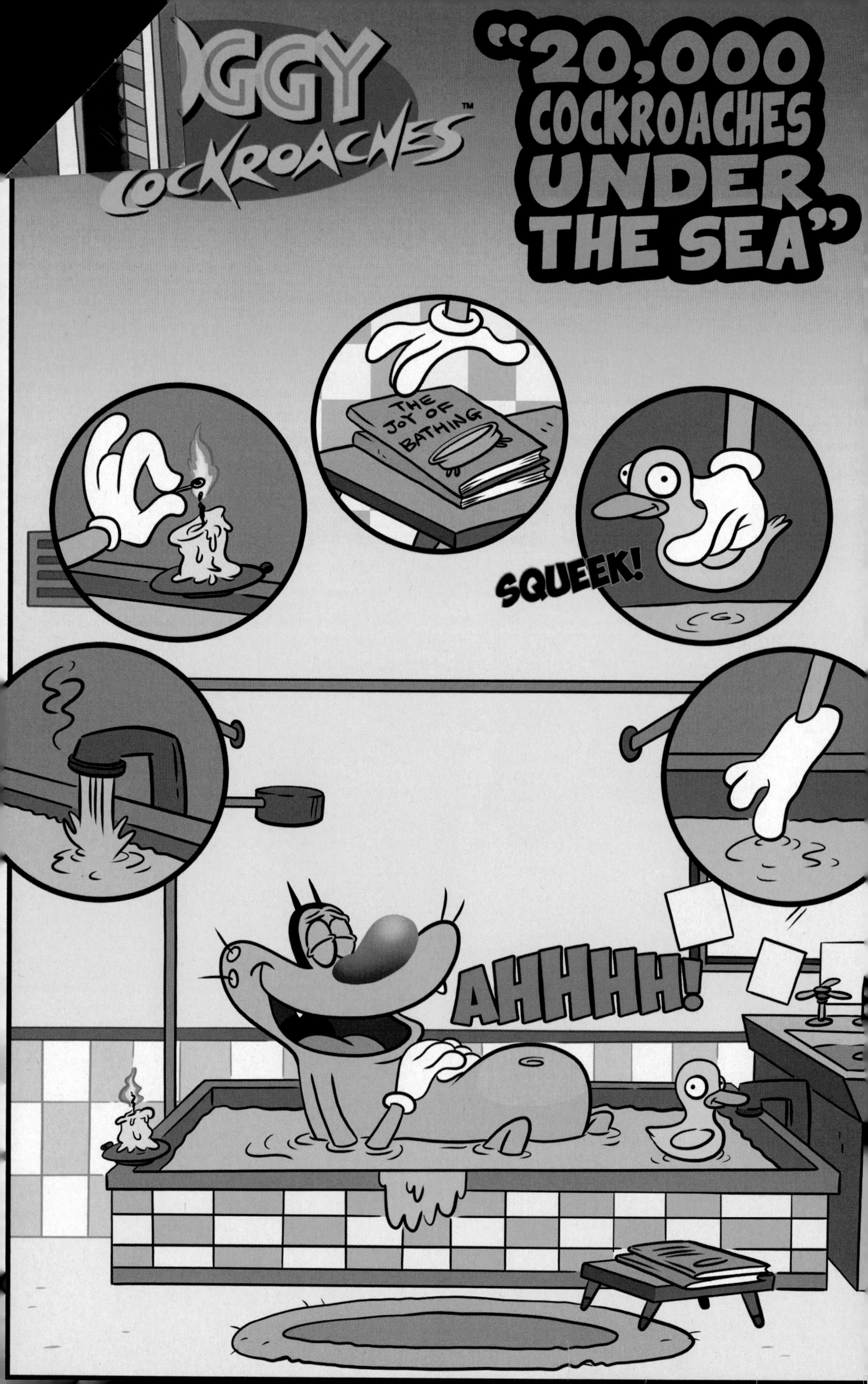
"20,000 COCKROACHES UNDER THE SEA"
THE JOY OF BATHING
SQUEEK!
AHHHH!

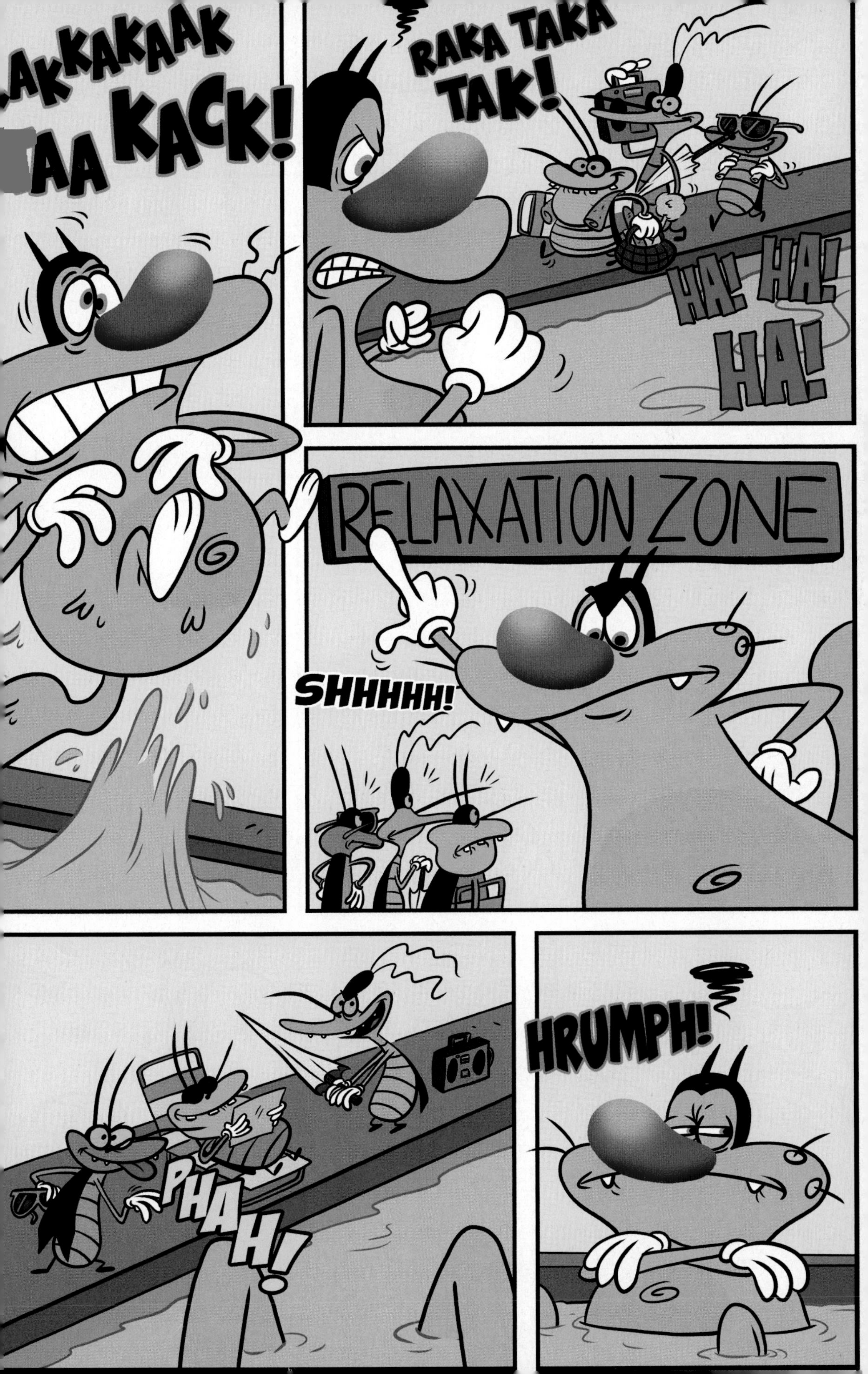
AKKAKAAK
AA KACK!
RAKA TAKA TAK!
HA! HA! HA!
RELAXATION ZONE
SHHHHH!
PHAH!
HRUMPH!

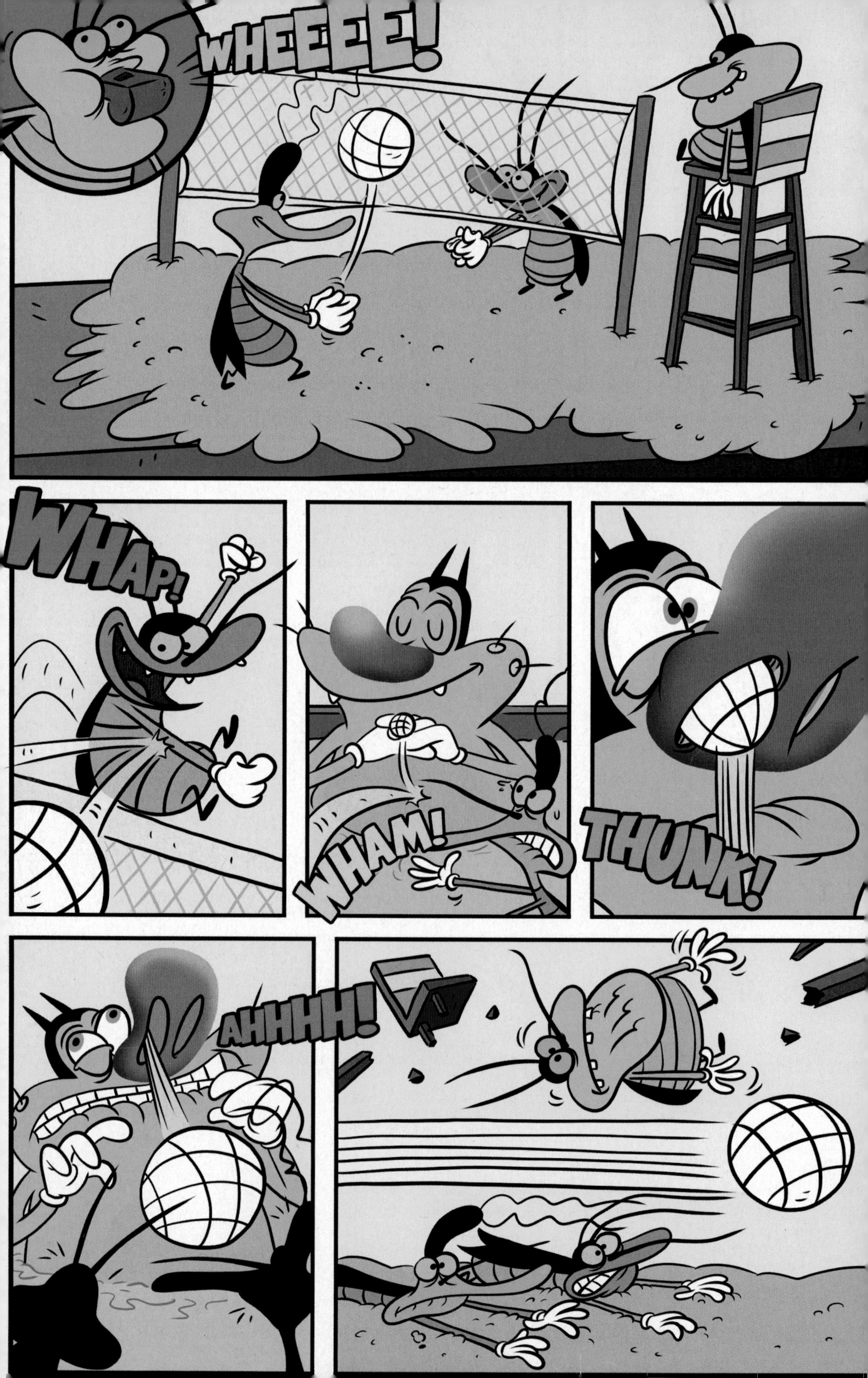
WHEEEEE!
WHAP!
WHAM!
THUNK!
AHHHH!

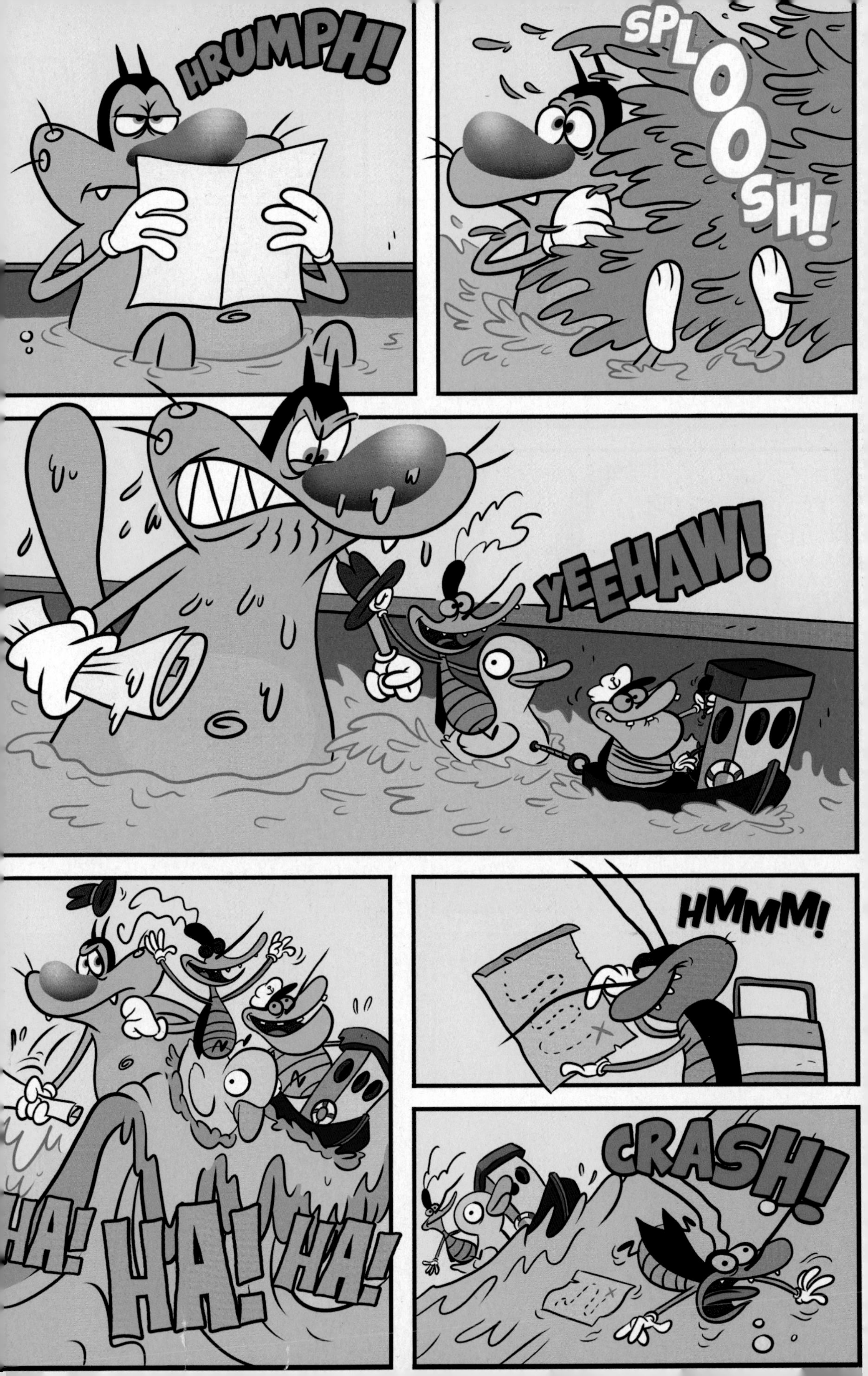
HRUMPH!
SPLOOOSH!
YEEHAW!
HA! HA! HA!
HMMM!
CRASH!

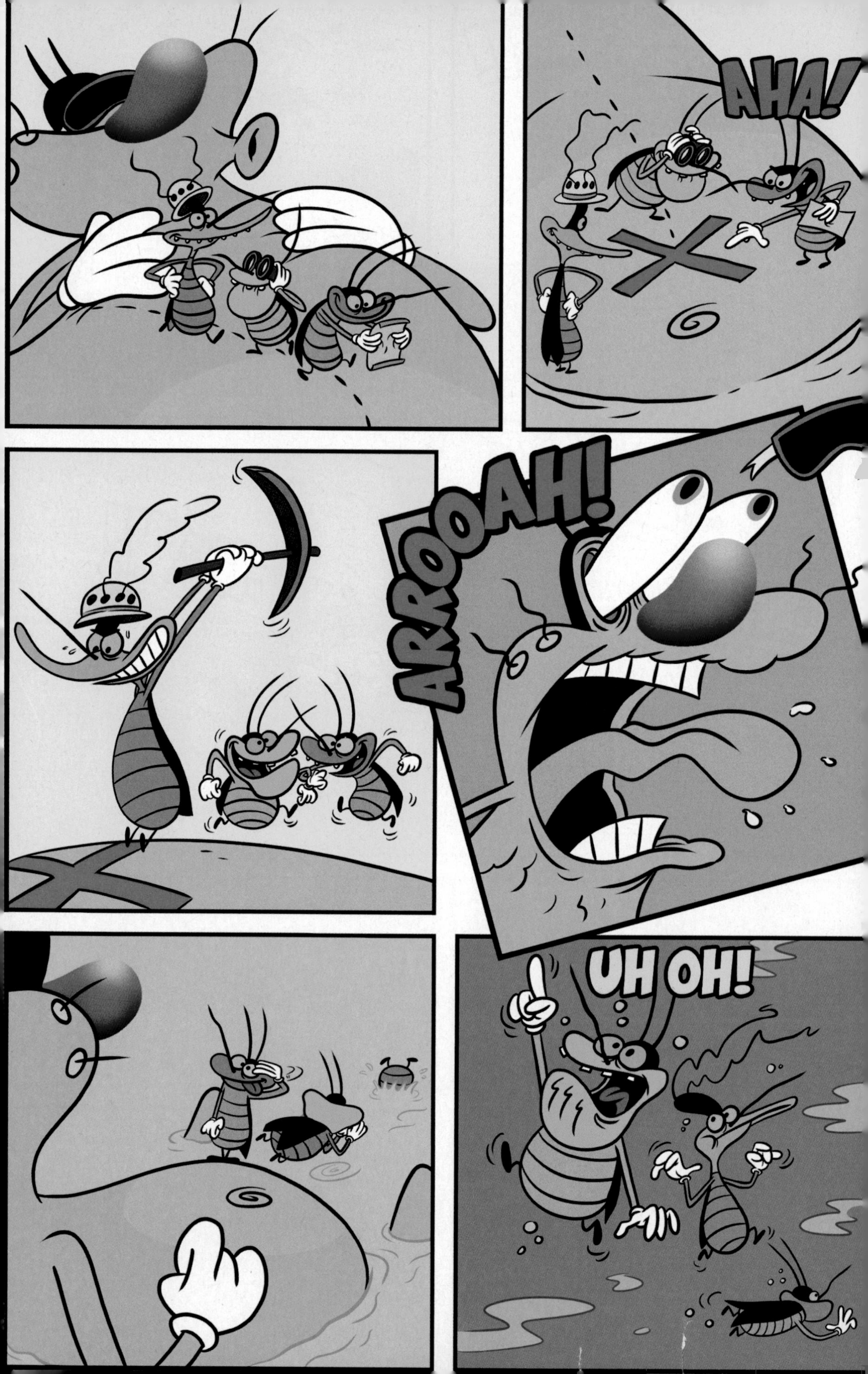
AHA!
ARROOAH!
UH OH!

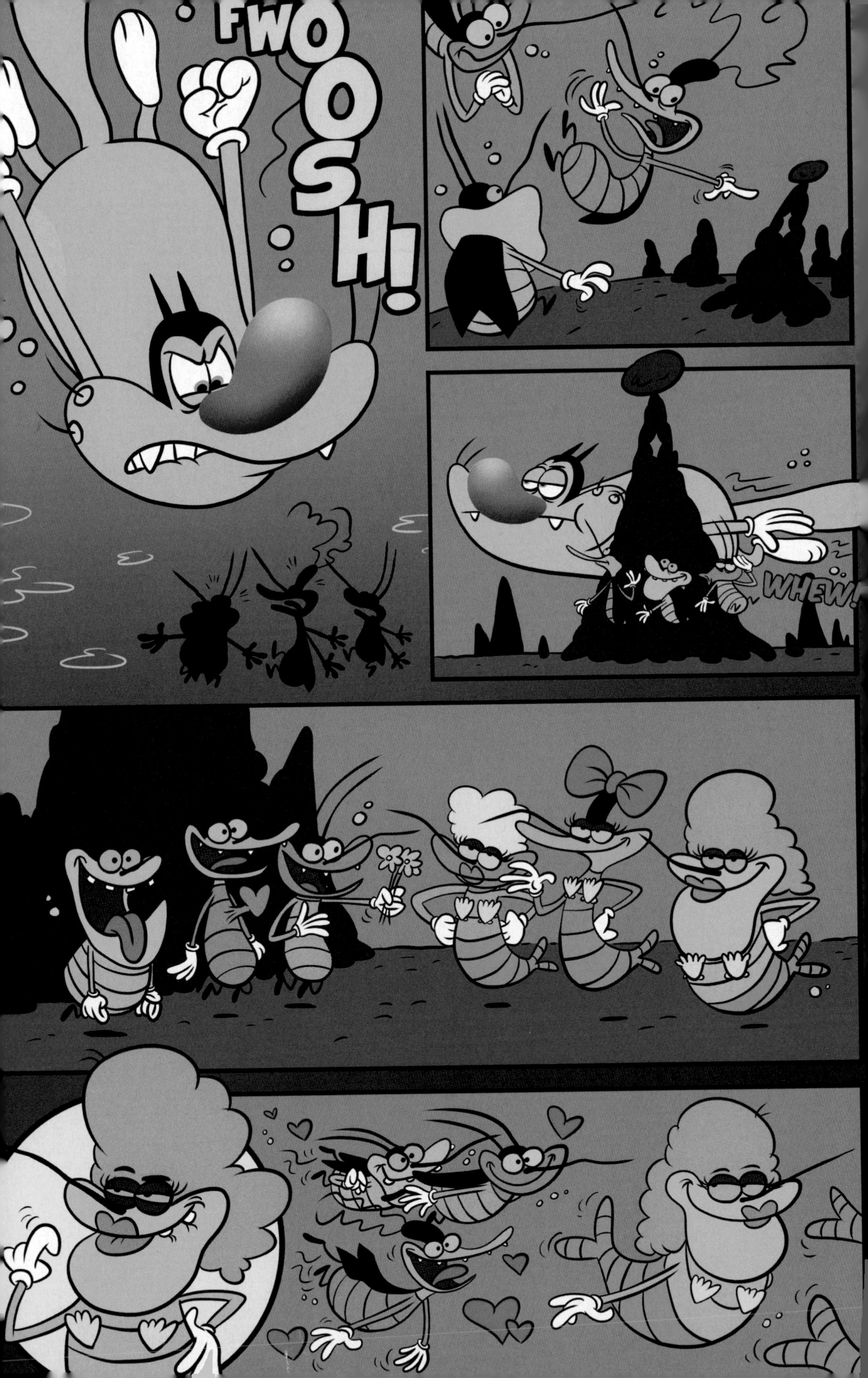
FWOOOSH!
WHEW!

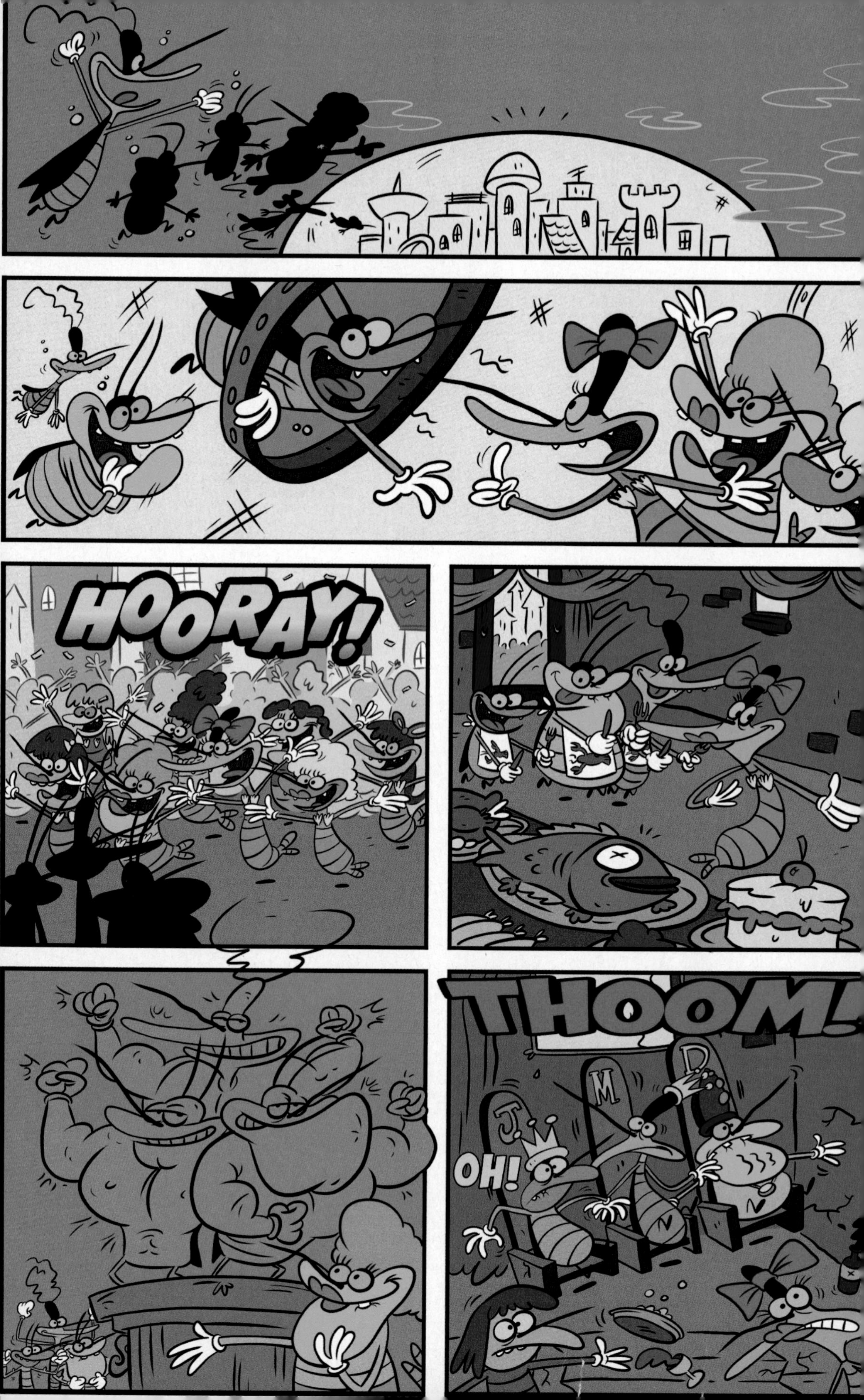
HOORAY!
THOOM!
OH!

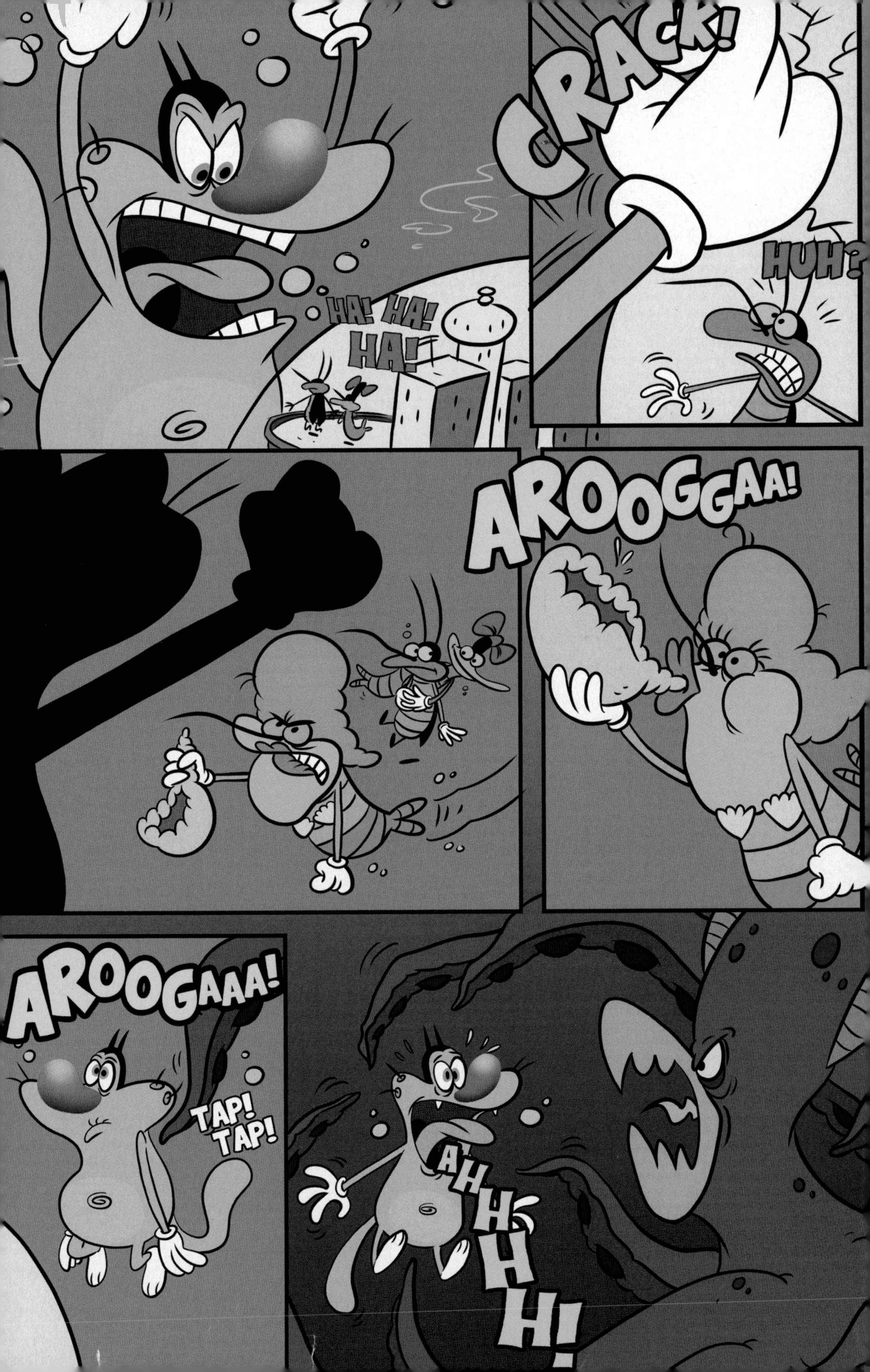
HA! HA!
HA!
CRACK!
HUH?
AROOGGAA!
AROOGAAA!
TAP!
TAP!
AHHHHH!

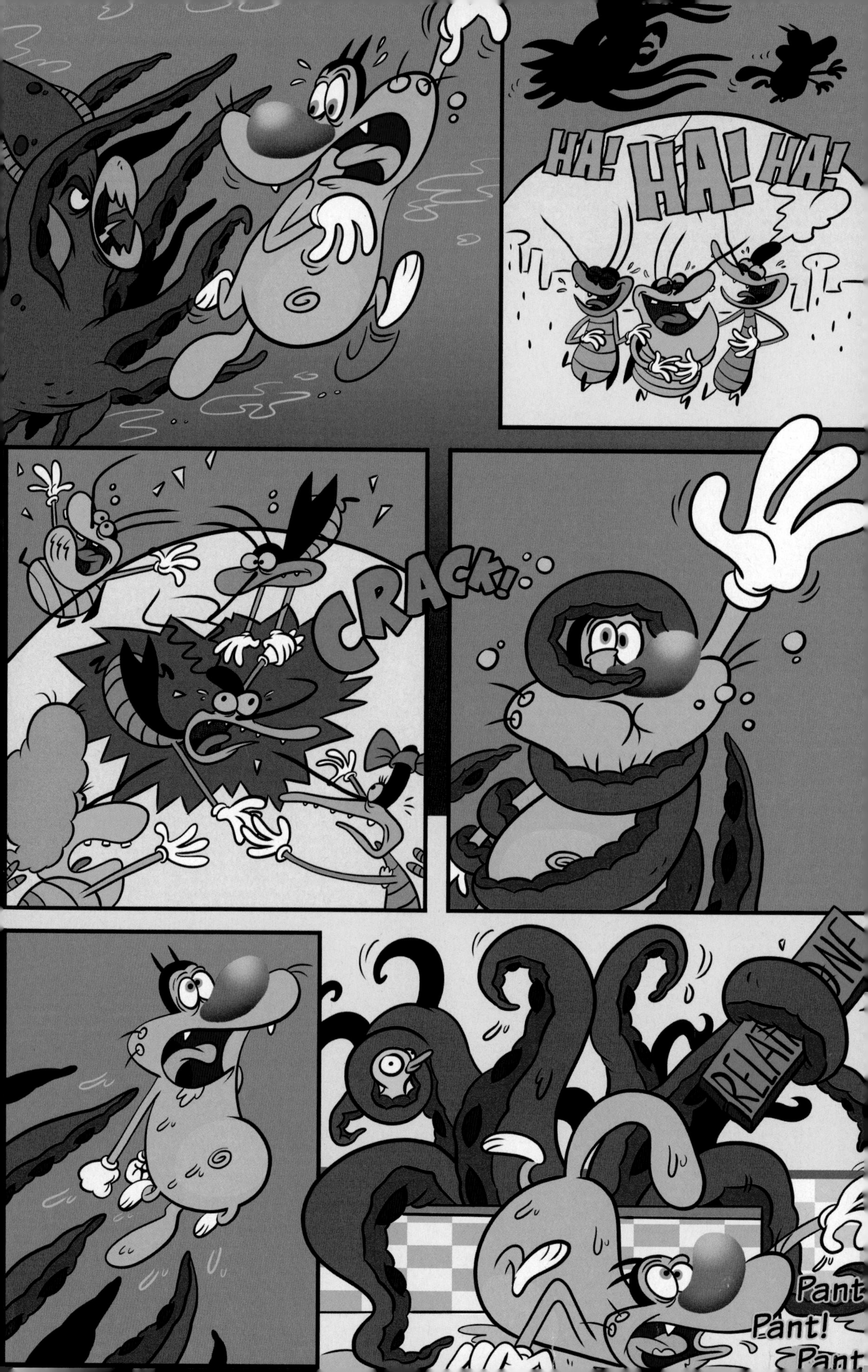

HA! HA! HA!
CRACK!
Pant
Pant!
Pant.

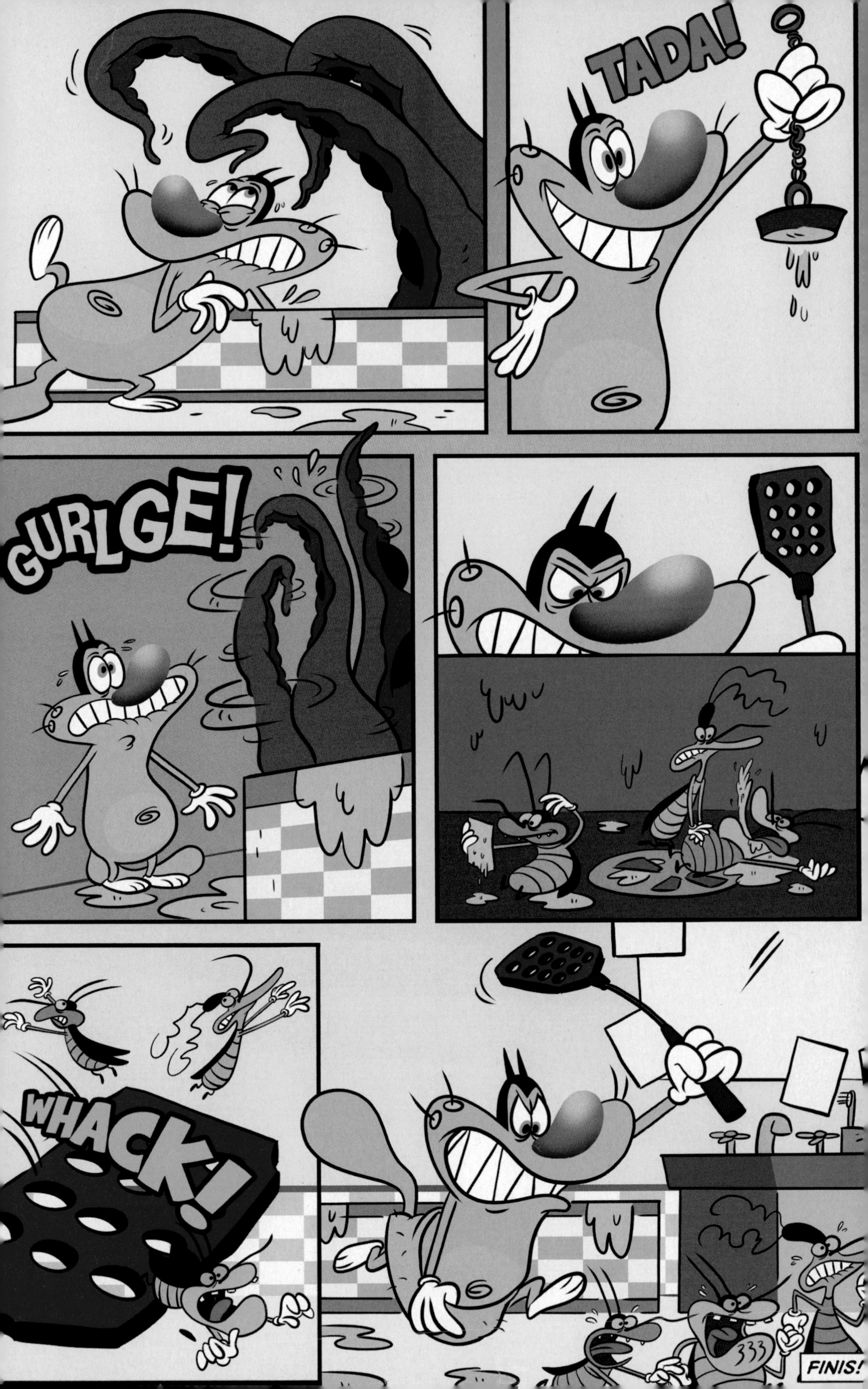
TADA!
GURLGE!
WHACK!
FINIS!

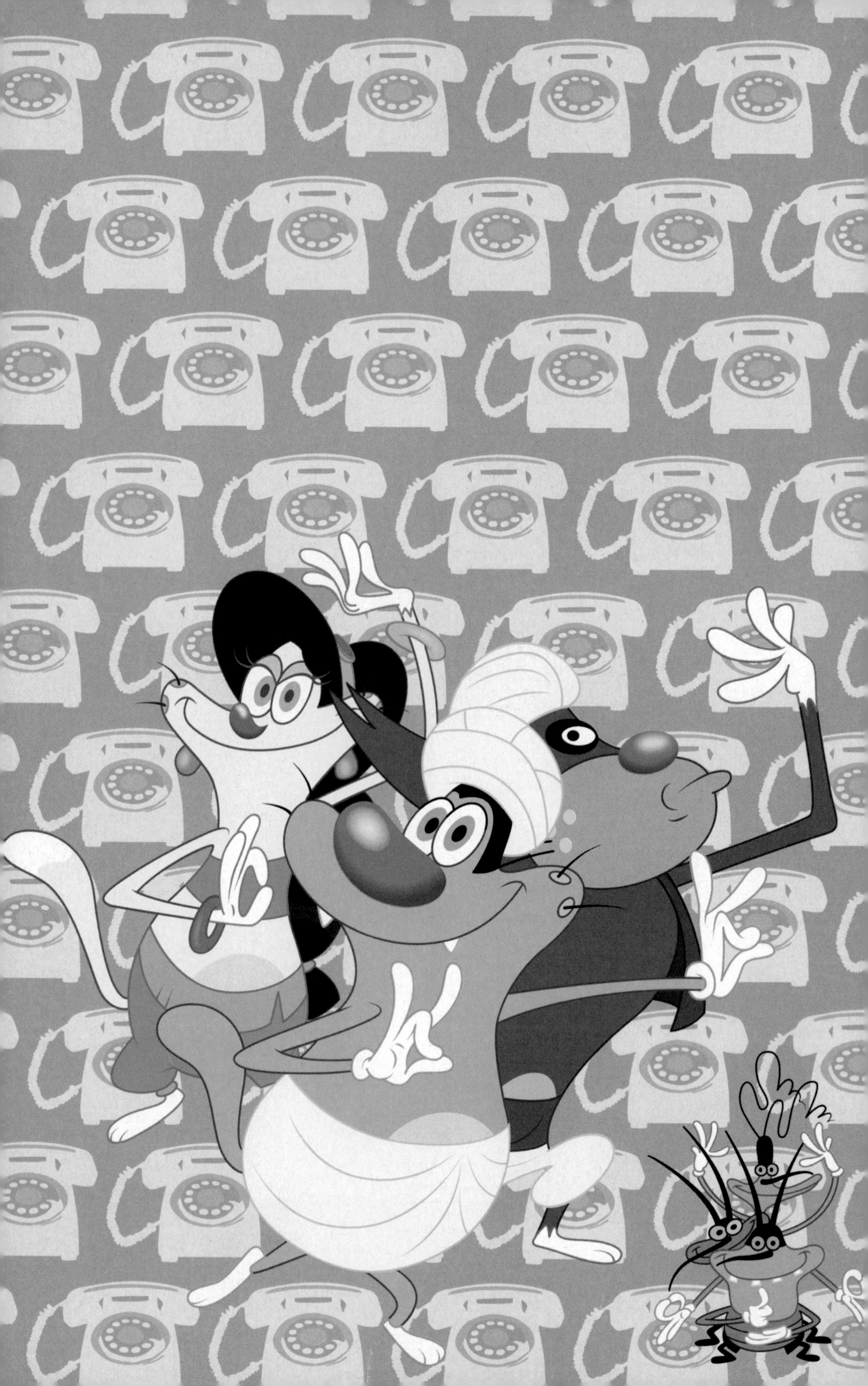

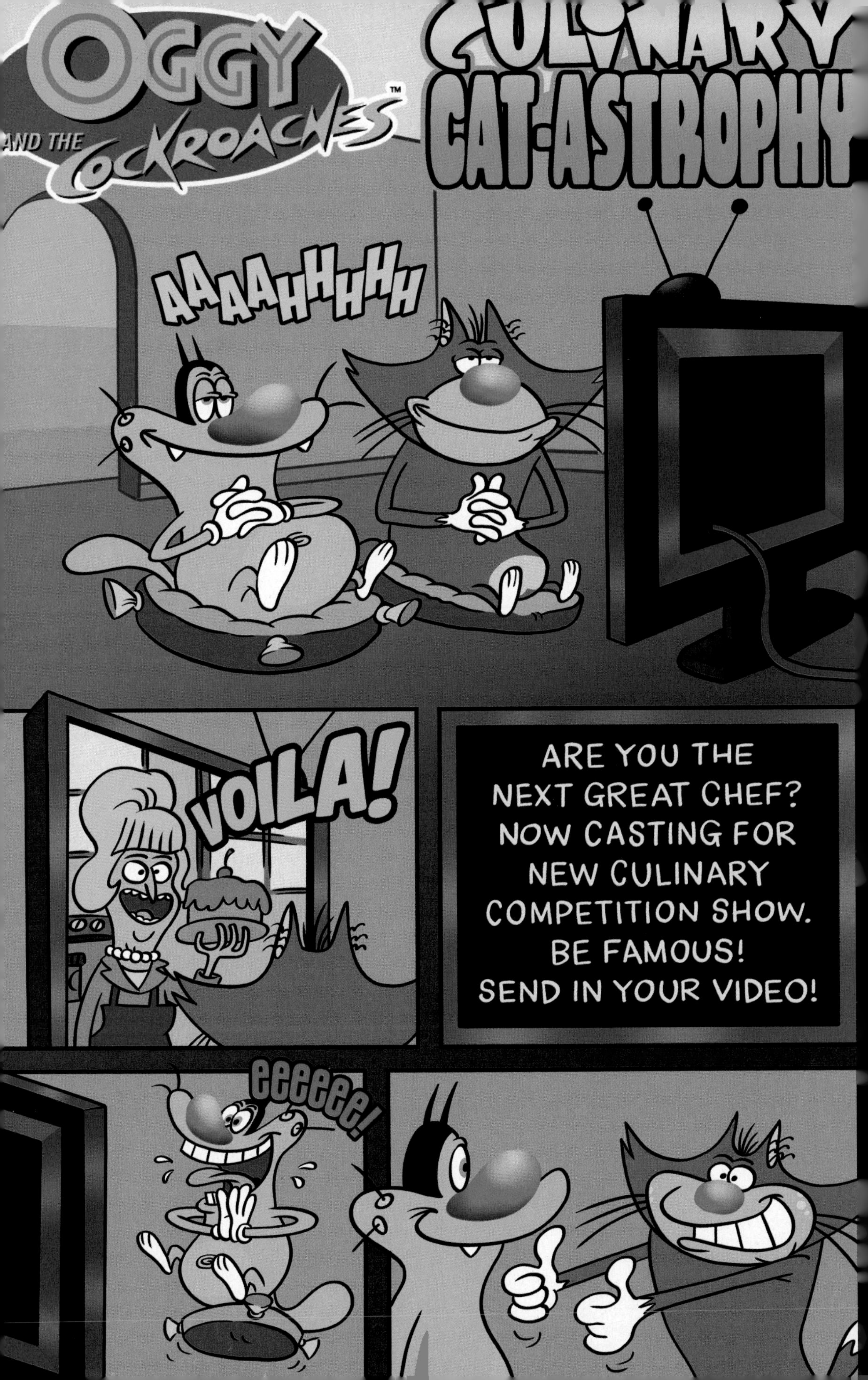
OGGY AND THE COCKROACHES™
CULINARY CAT-ASTROPHY
AAAAHHHHH
VOILA!
ARE YOU THE NEXT GREAT CHEF? NOW CASTING FOR NEW CULINARY COMPETITION SHOW. BE FAMOUS! SEND IN YOUR VIDEO!
eeeeee!

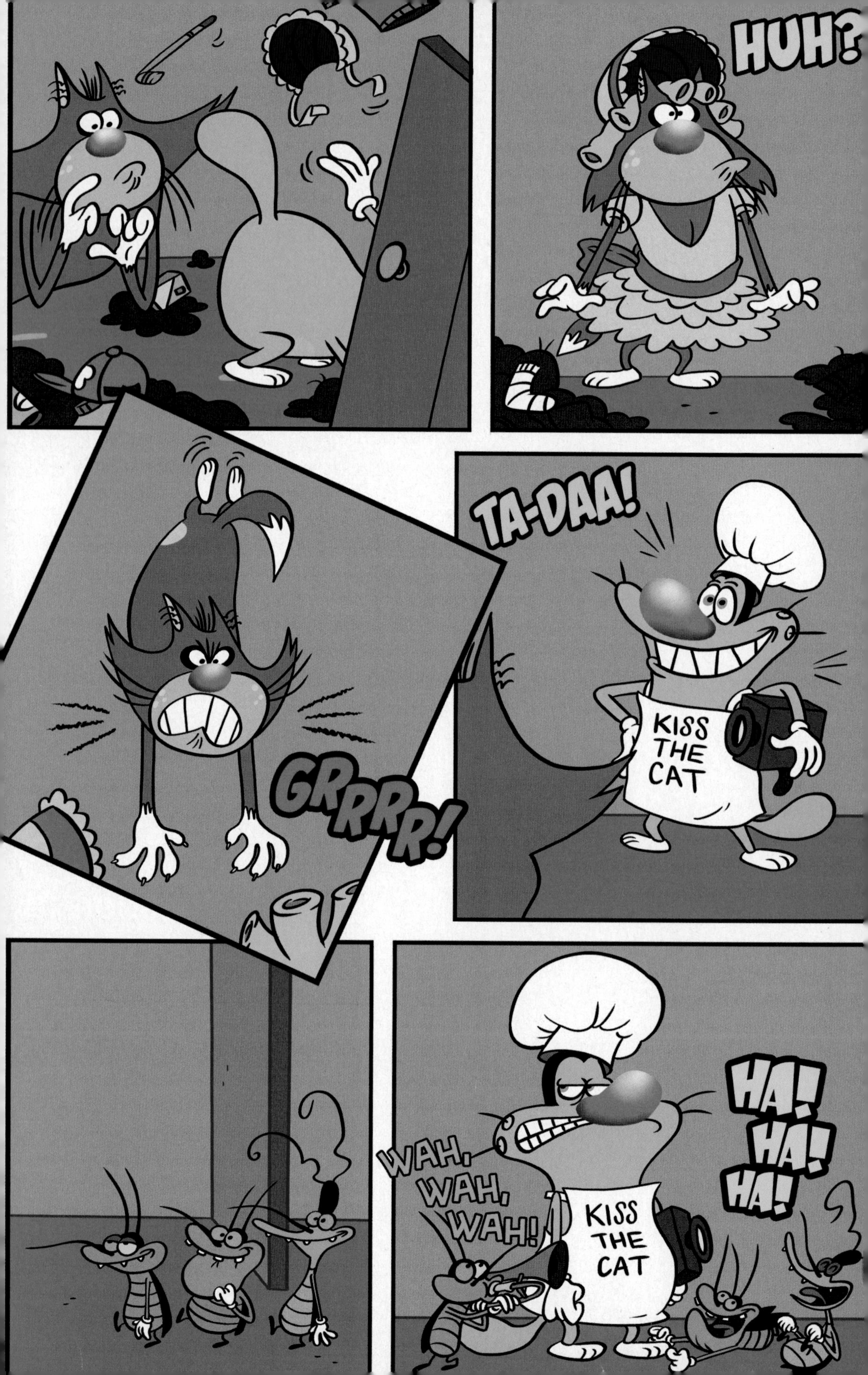
HUH?
GRRRRR!
TA-DAA!
KISS THE CAT
WAH, WAH, WAH!
KISS THE CAT
HA! HA! HA!

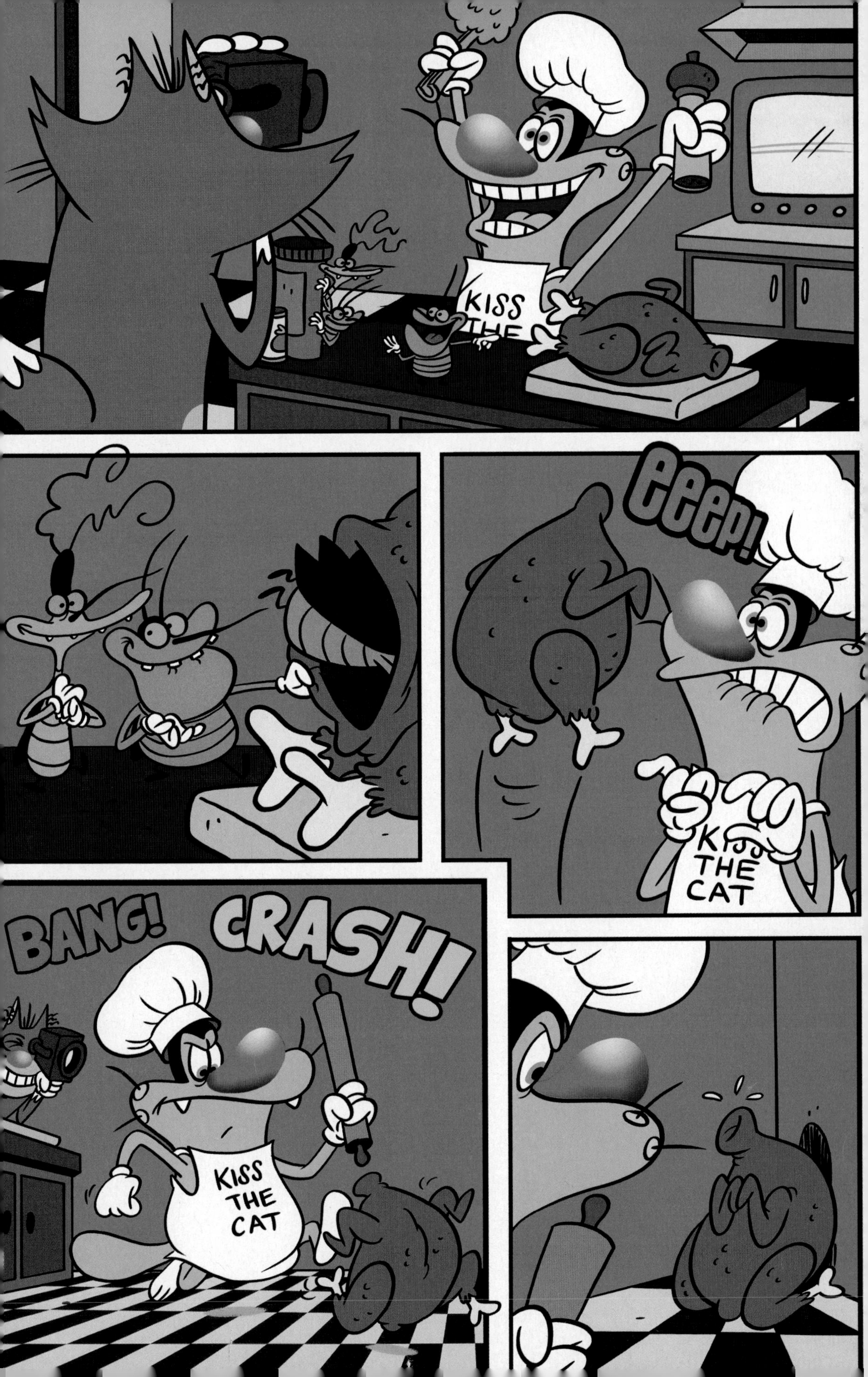

KISS THE
eeep!
KISS THE CAT
BANG!
CRASH!
KISS THE CAT

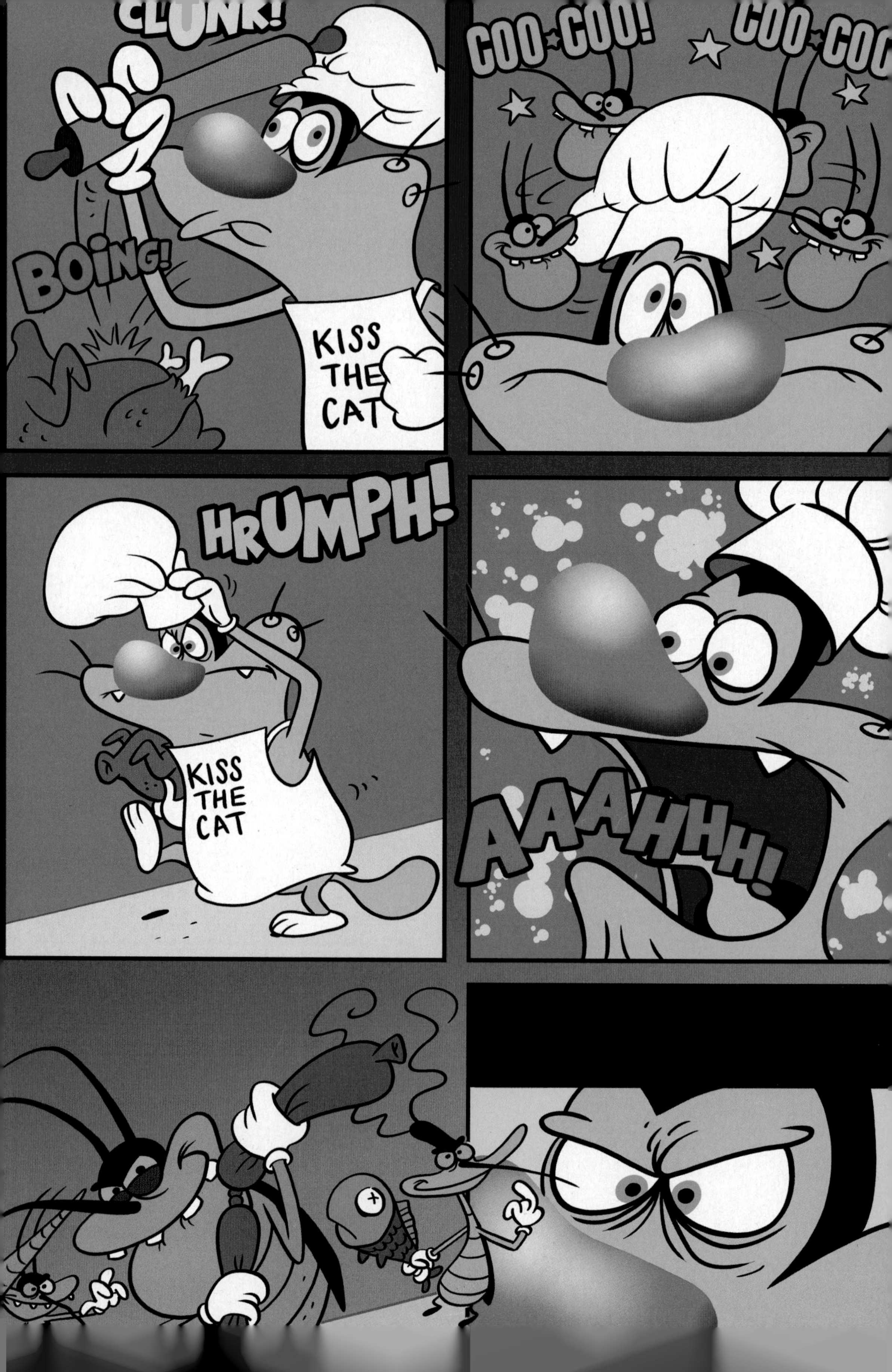
CLUNK!
BOING!
KISS THE CAT
COO-COO!
COO-COO
HRUMPH!
KISS THE CAT
AAAHHH!

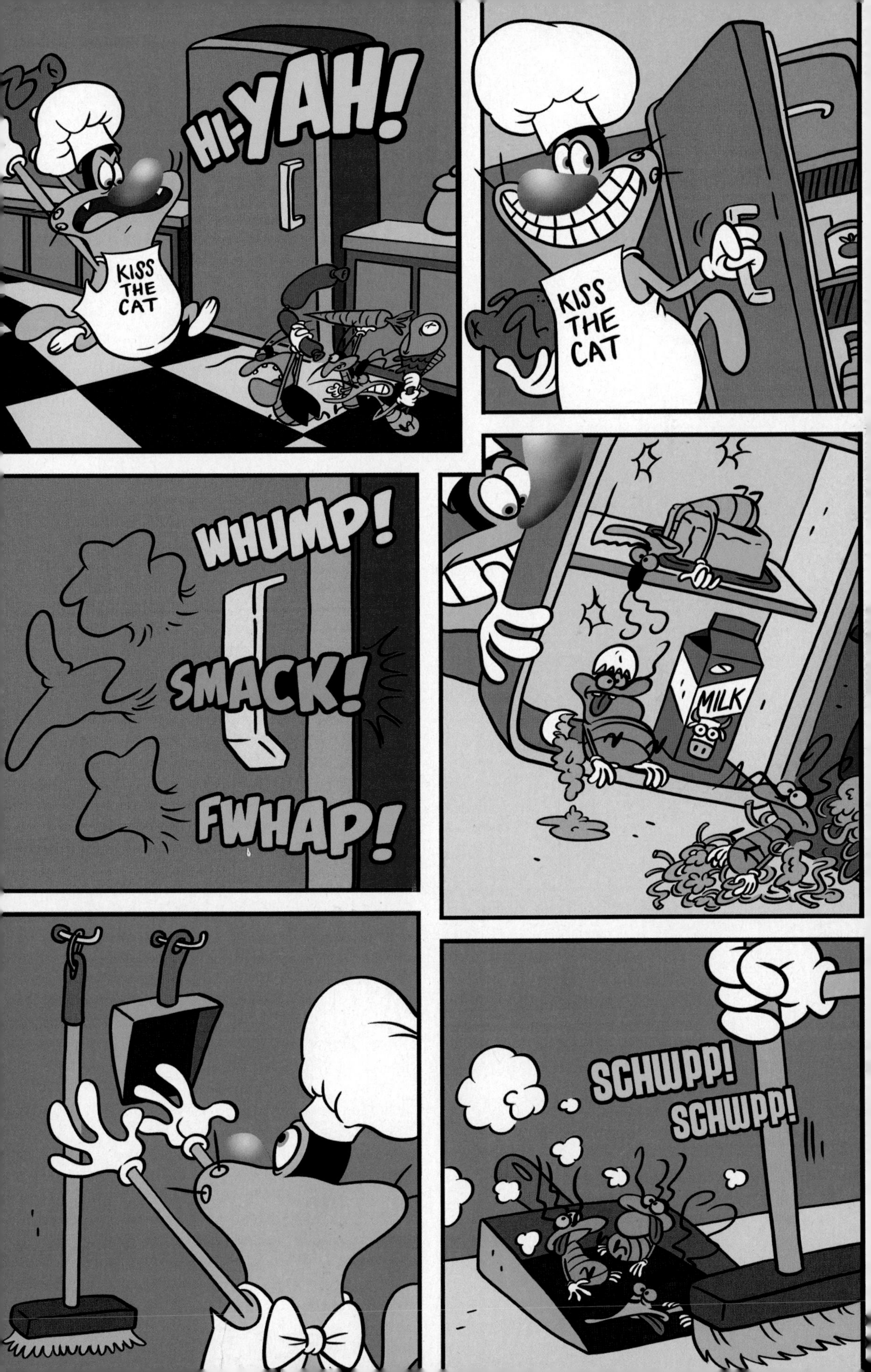
HI-YAH!
KISS THE CAT
KISS THE CAT
WHUMP!
SMACK!
FWHAP!
MILK
SCHWPP!
SCHWPP!

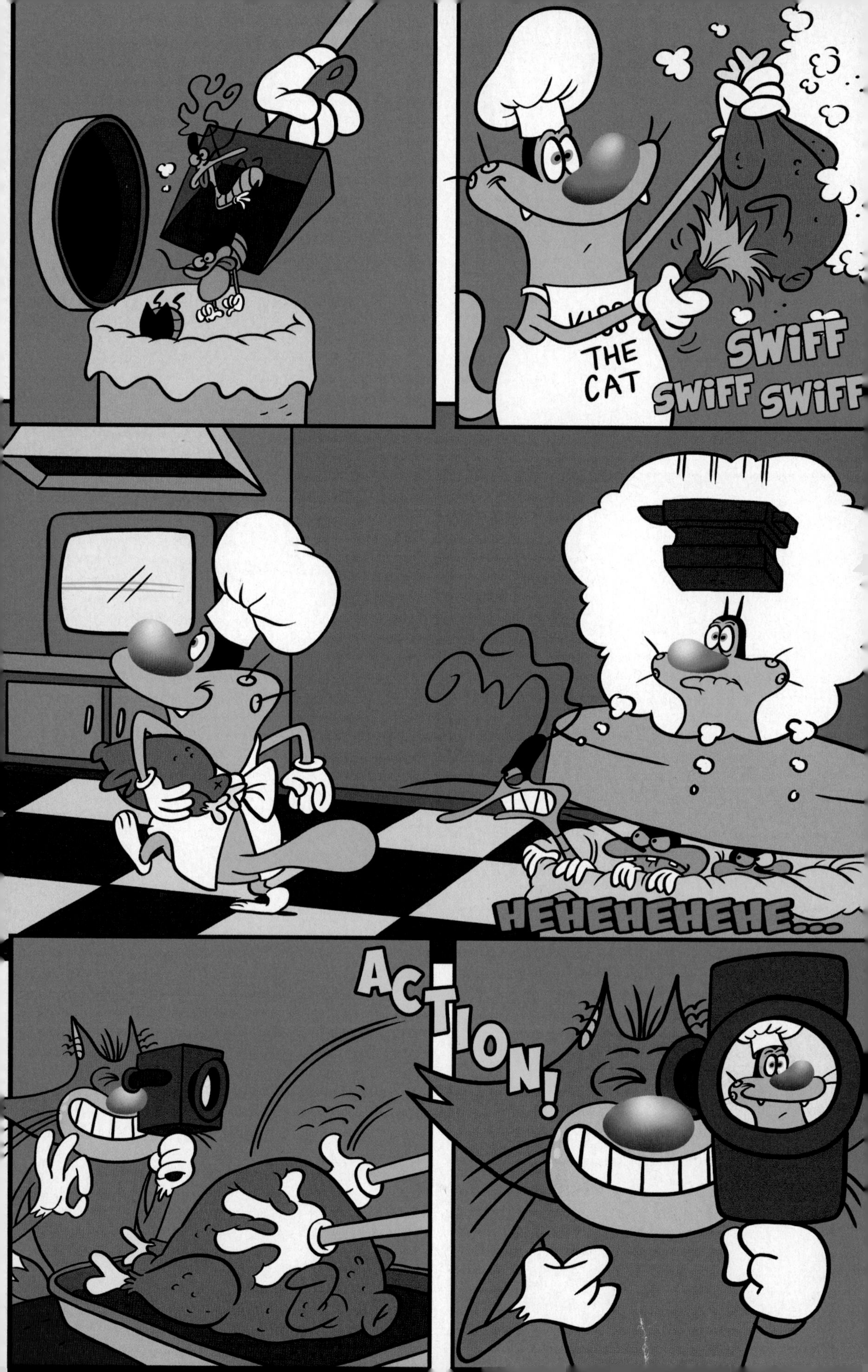
THE CAT
SWIFF
SWIFF SWIFF
HEHEHEHEHEHE...
ACTION!

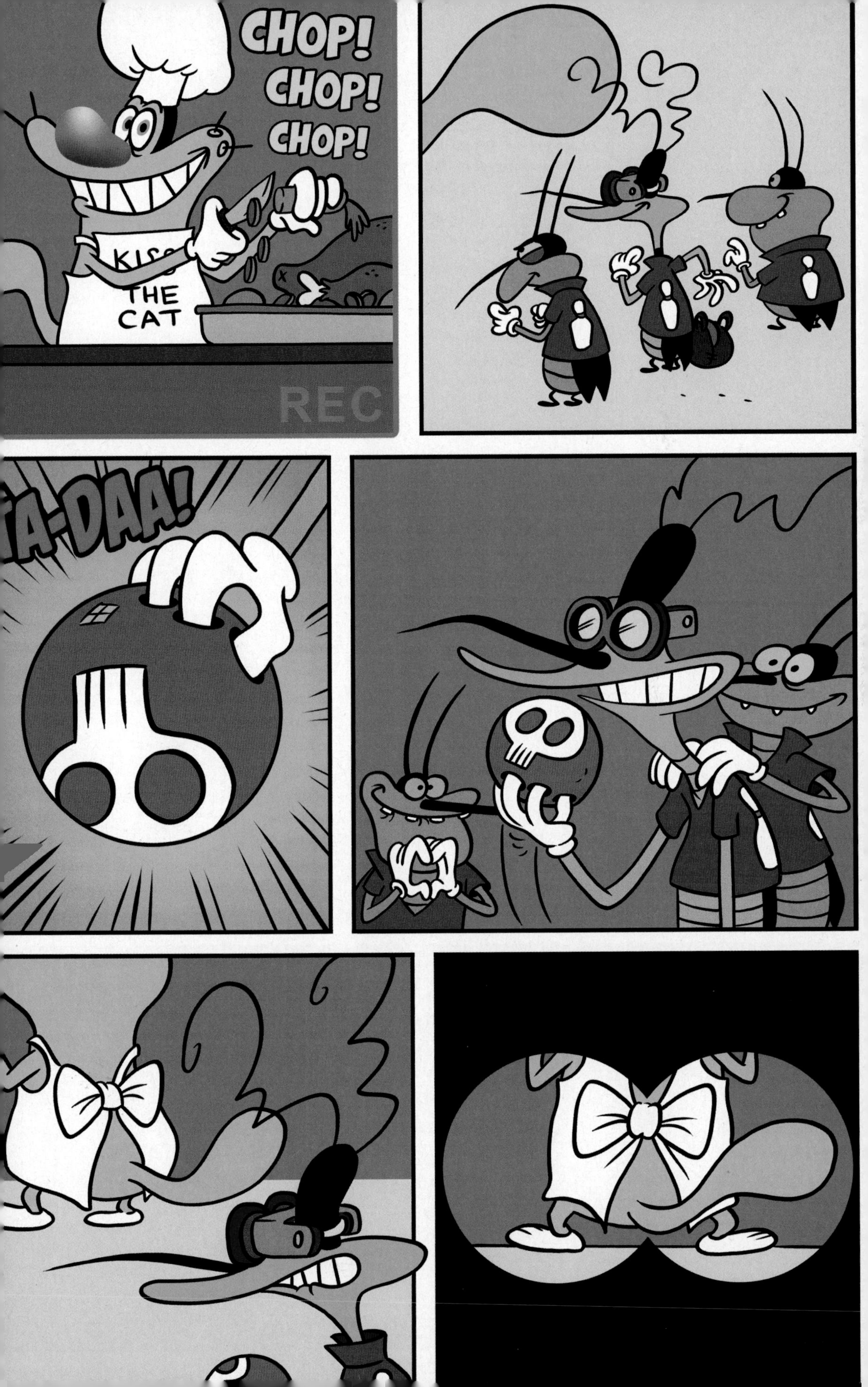
CHOP! CHOP! CHOP!
KISS THE CAT
REC
TA-DAA!

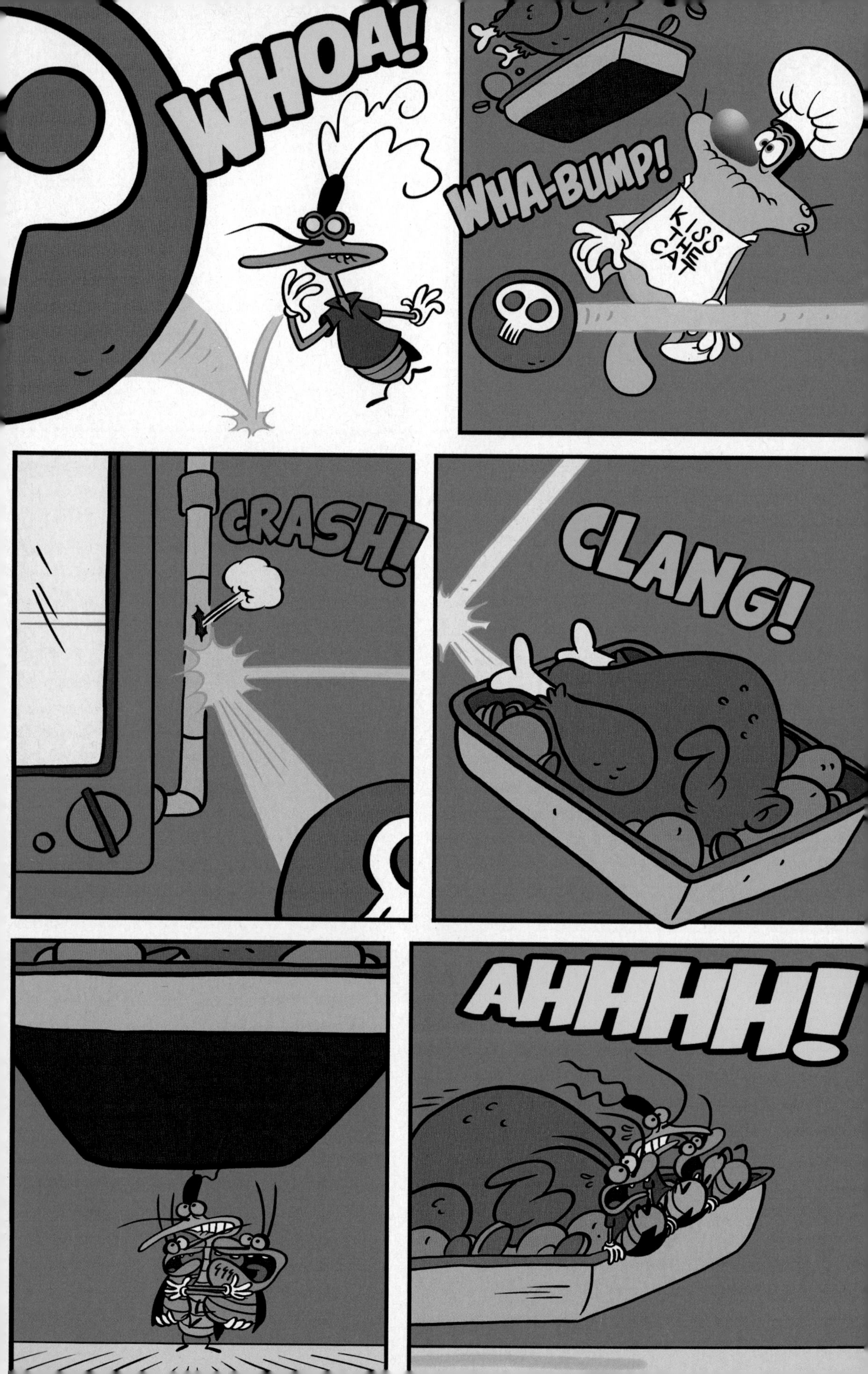
WHOA!
WHA-BUMP!
KISS THE CAT
CRASH!
CLANG!
AHHHHH!

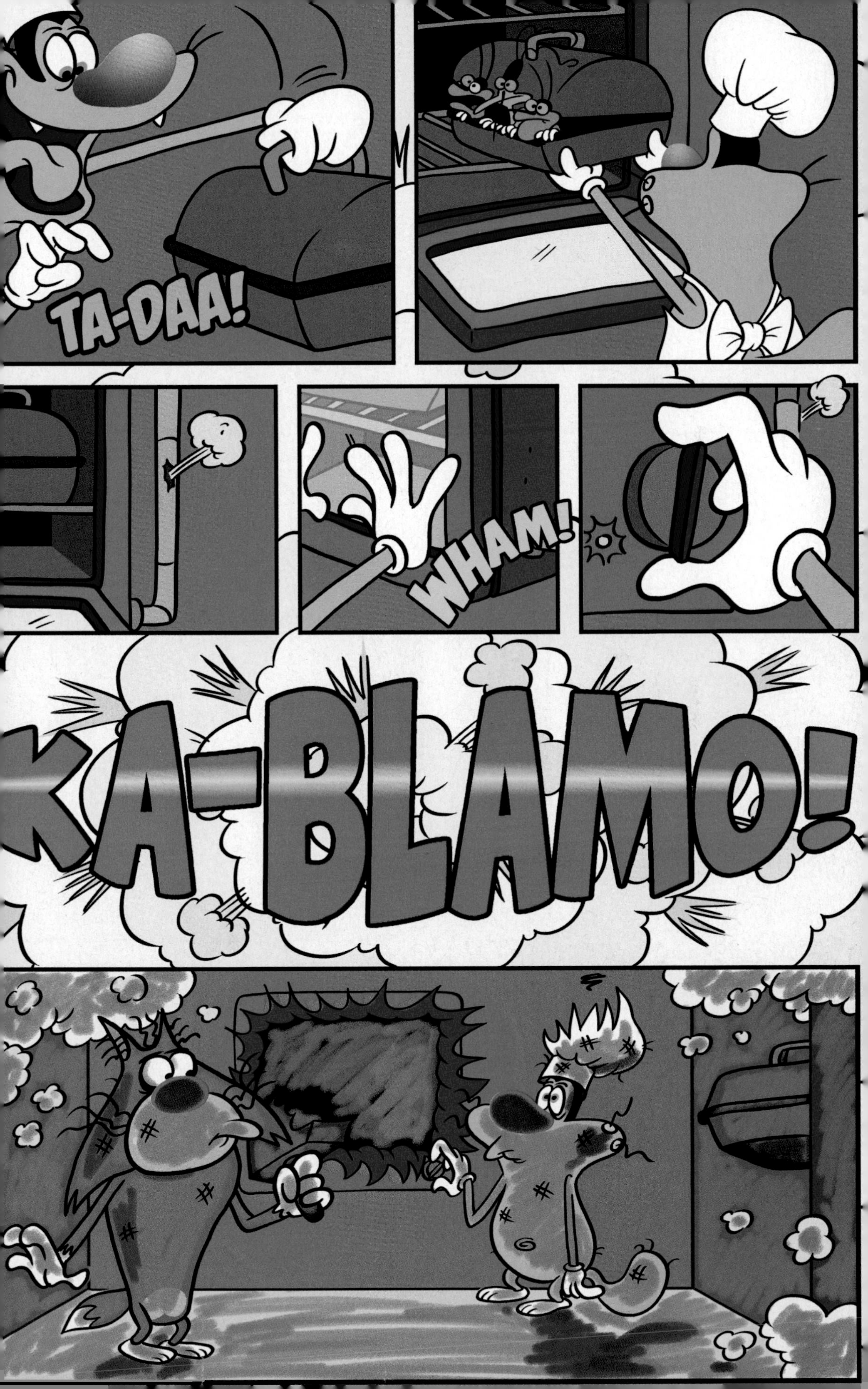
TA-DAA!
WHAM!
KA-BLAMO!

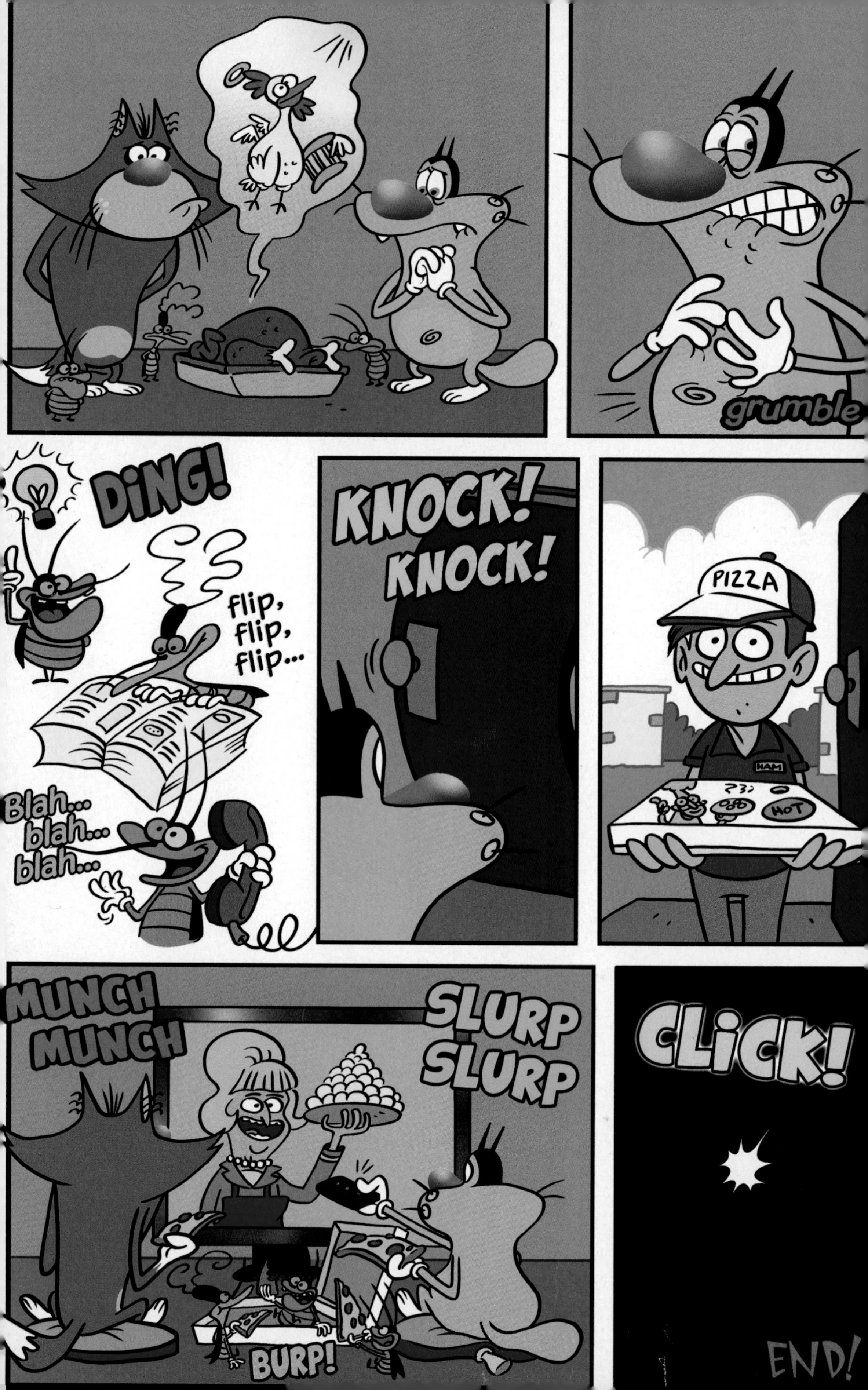
grumble
DiNG!
flip, flip, flip...
Blah... blah... blah...
KNOCK! KNOCK!
PIZZA
HOT
MUNCH MUNCH
SLURP SLURP
BURP!
CLiCK!
END!

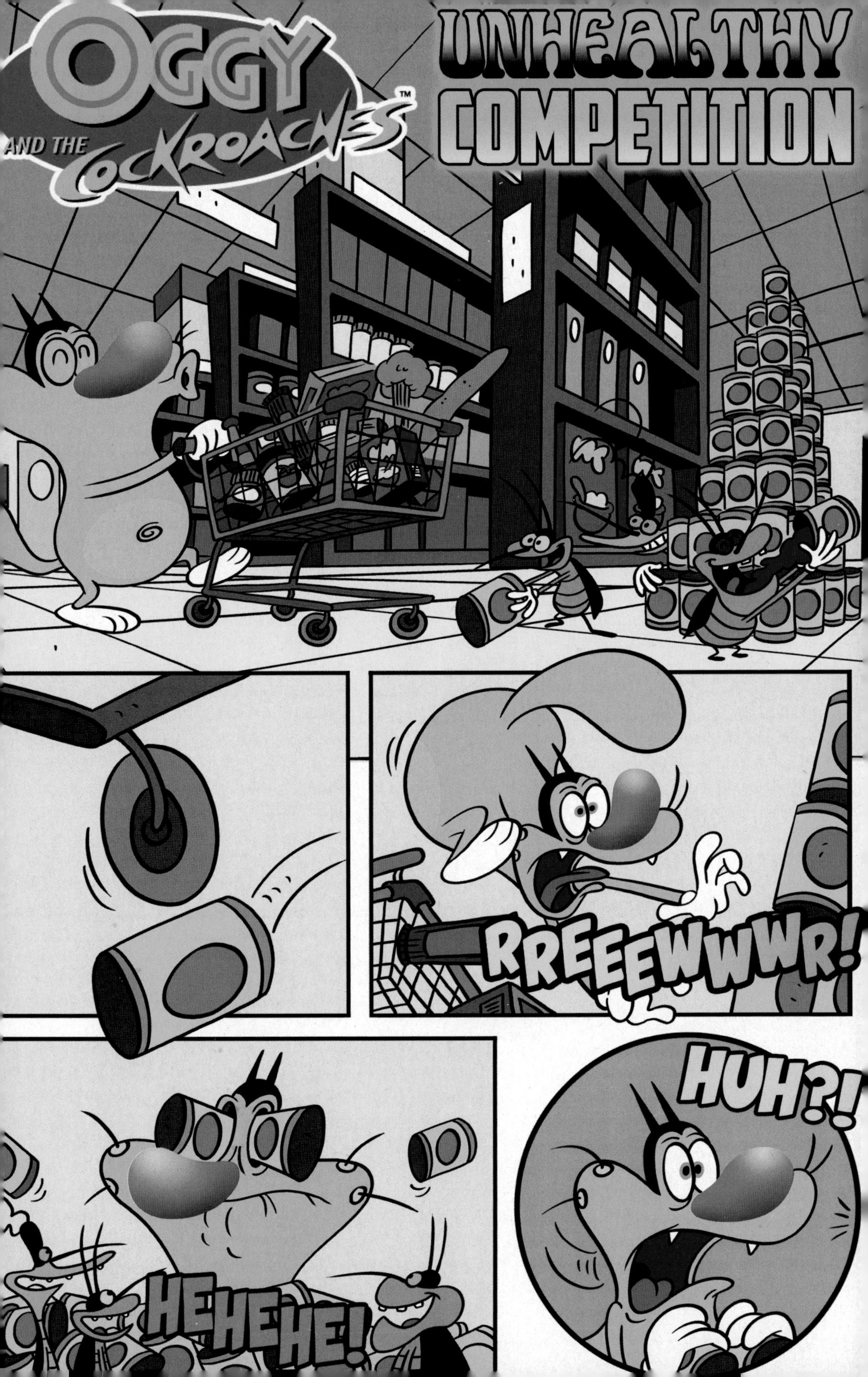
OGGY AND THE COCKROACHES™
UNHEALTHY COMPETITION
RREEEEWWWR!
HEHEHEHE!
HUH?!

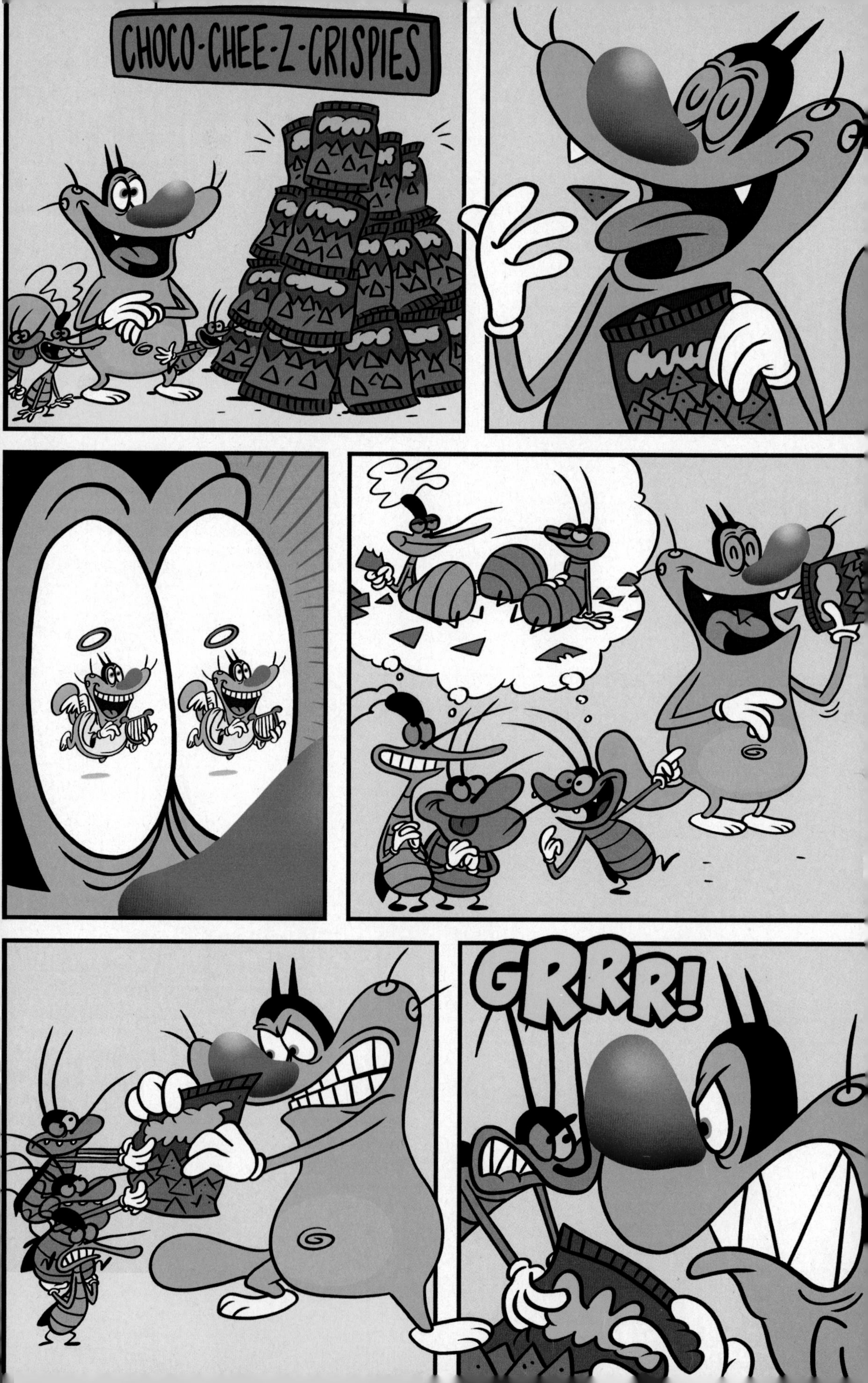
CHOCO-CHEE-Z-CRISPIES
GRRR!

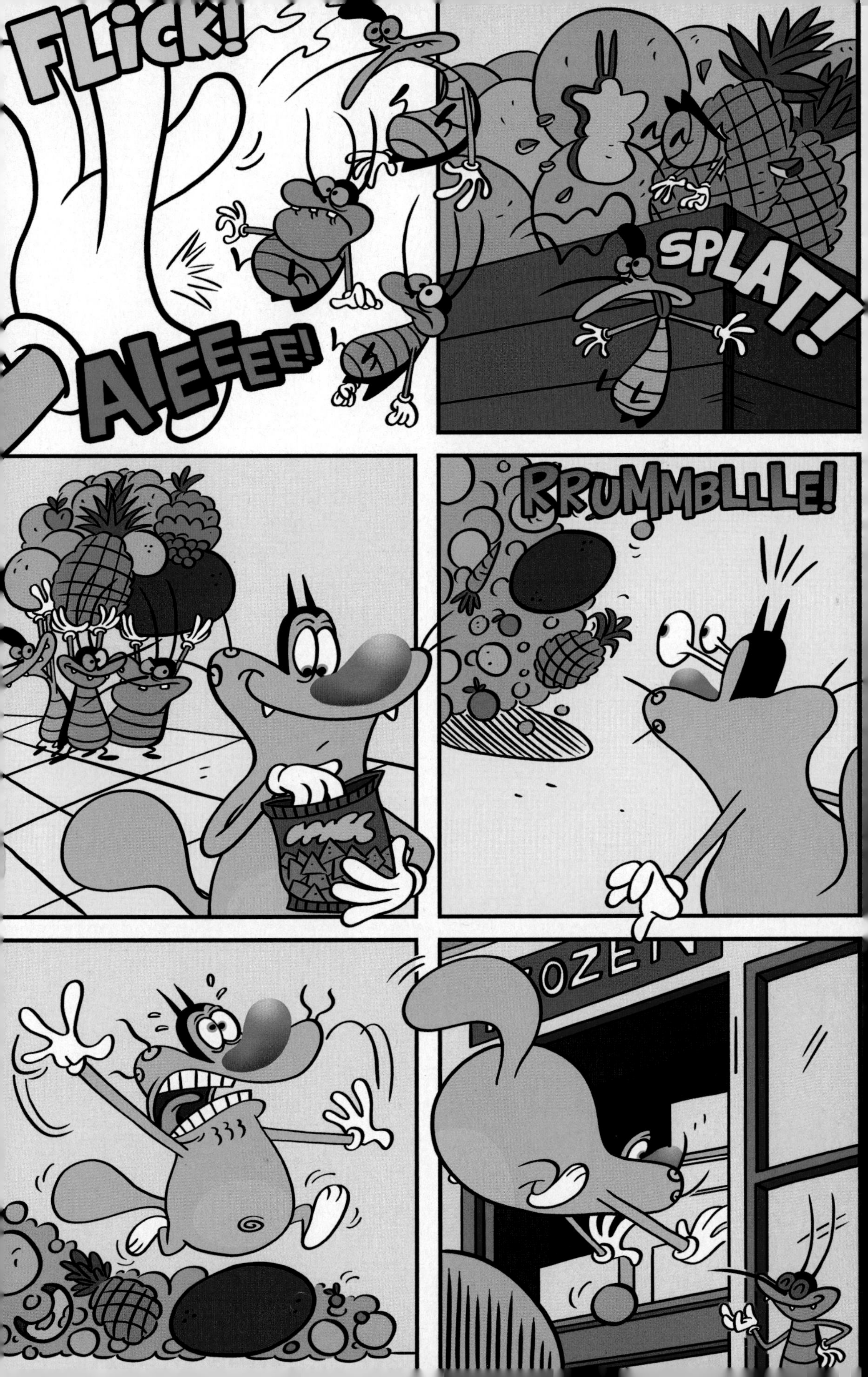
FLICK!
AIEEEEE!
SPLAT!
RRUMMBLLLE!

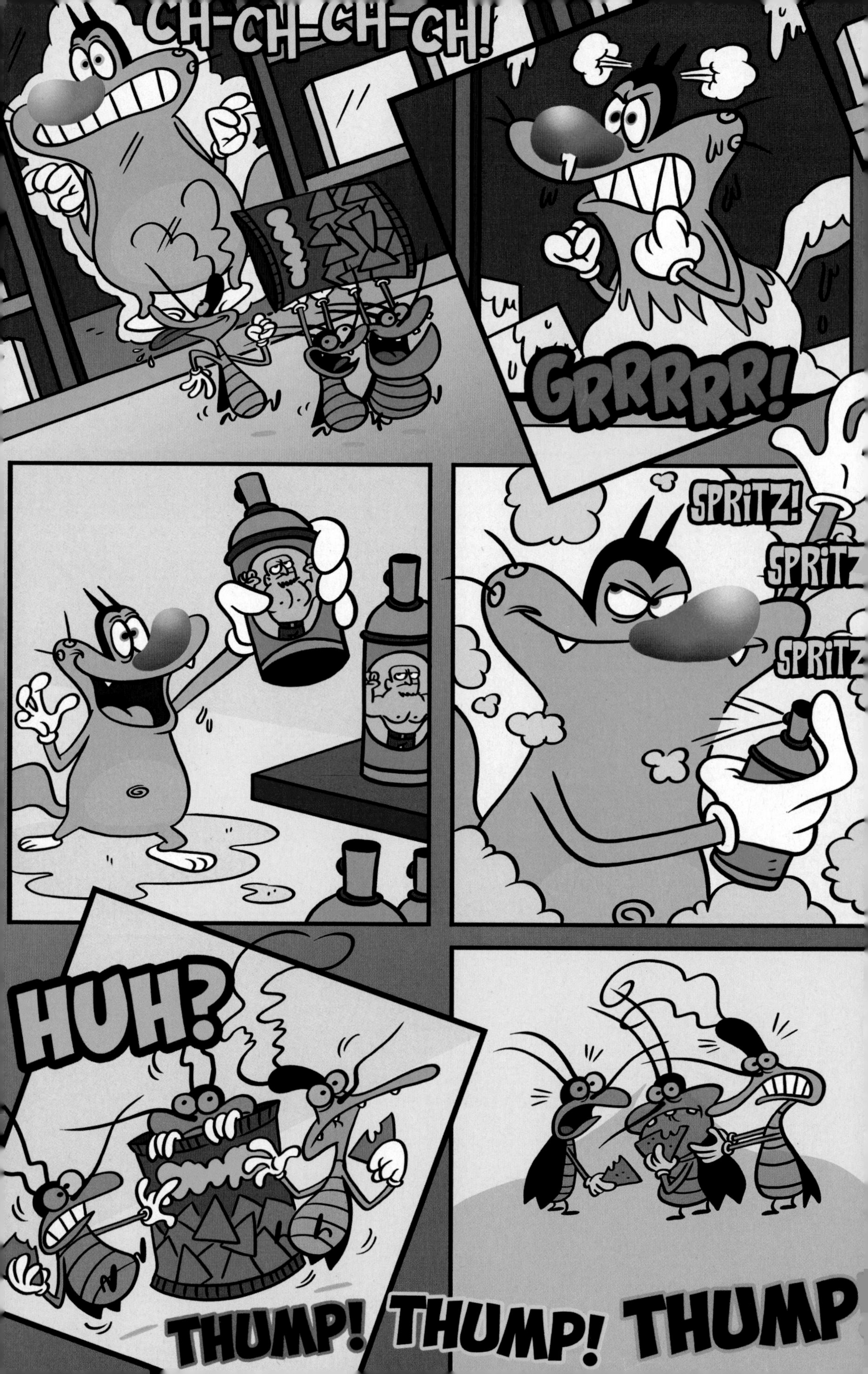
CH-CH-CH-CH!
GRRRRRR!
SPRITZ!
SPRITZ
SPRITZ
HUH?
THUMP!
THUMP!
THUMP

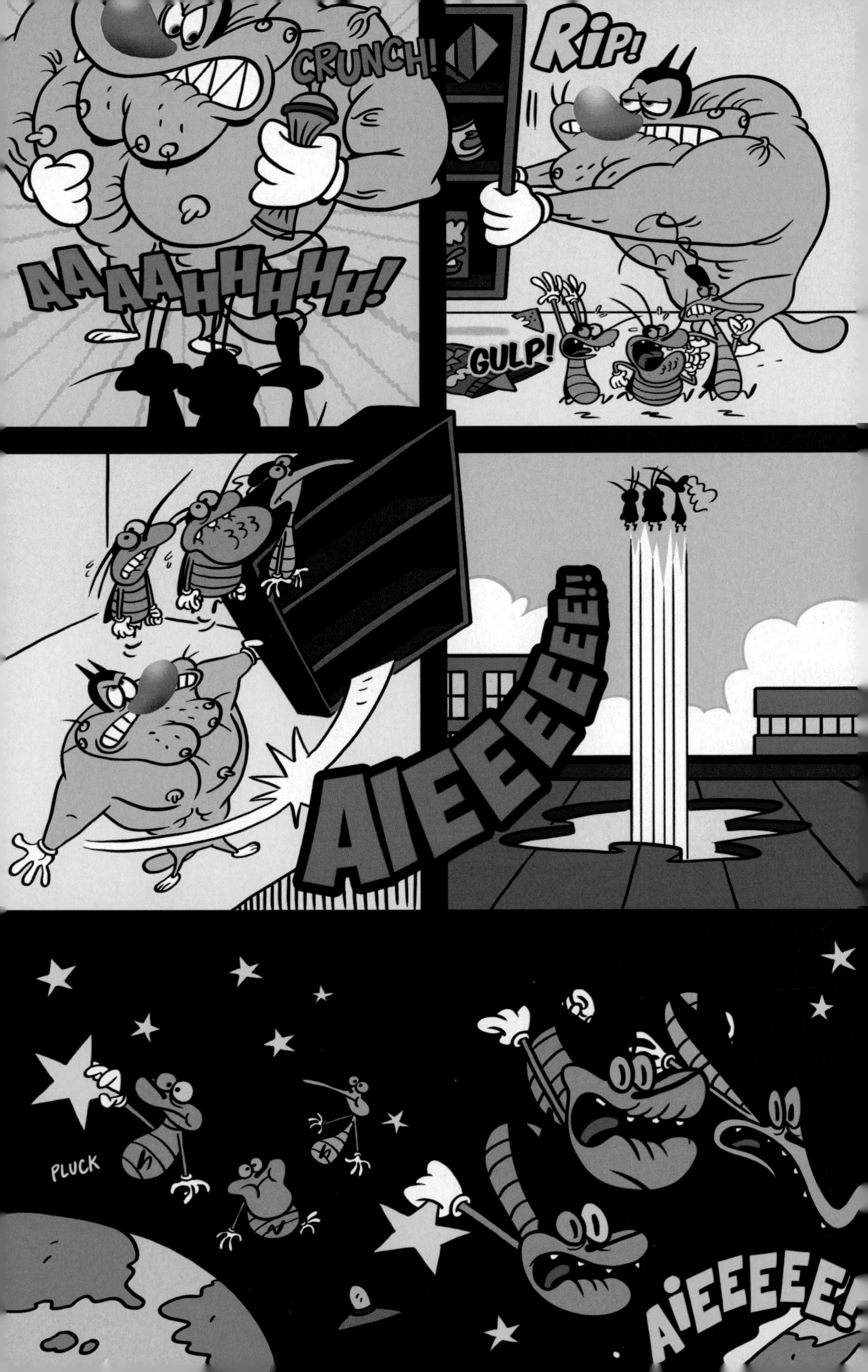
CRUNCH!
AAAAHHHHH!
RIP!
GULP!
AIEEEEEE!
PLUCK
AIEEEEE!

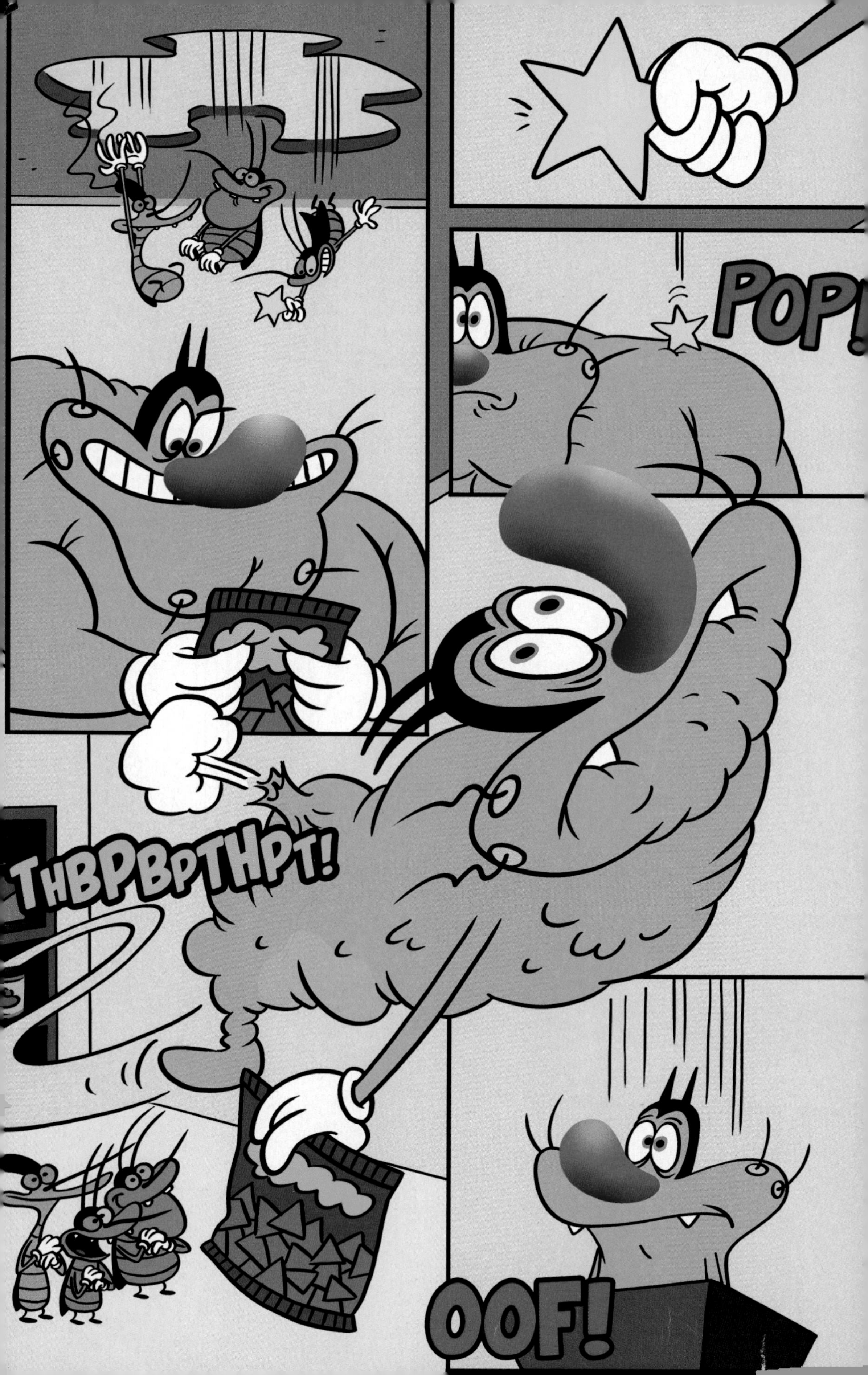
POP!
THBPBPTHPT!
OOF!

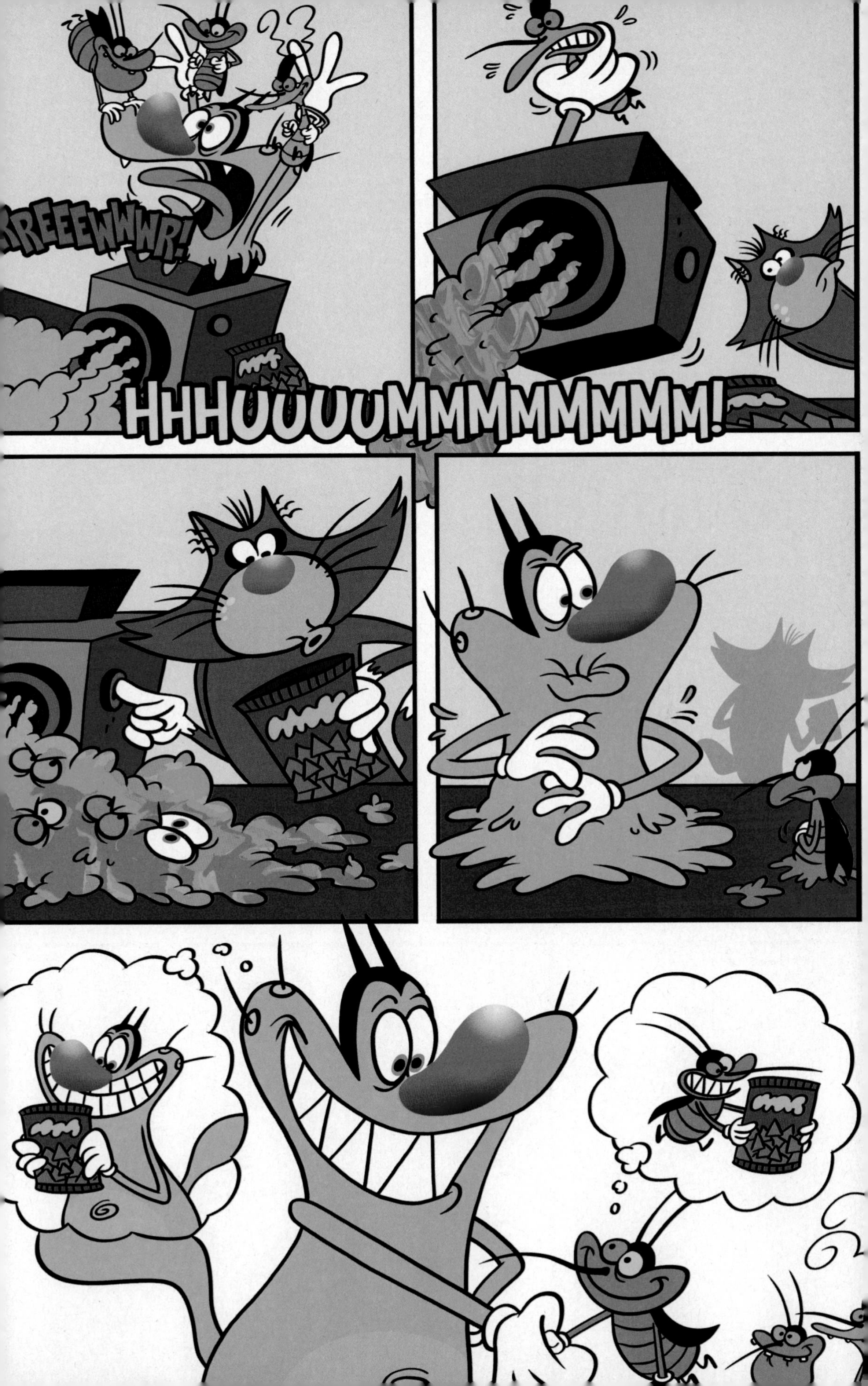
REEEWWWR!
HHHUUUUUMMMMMMMM!

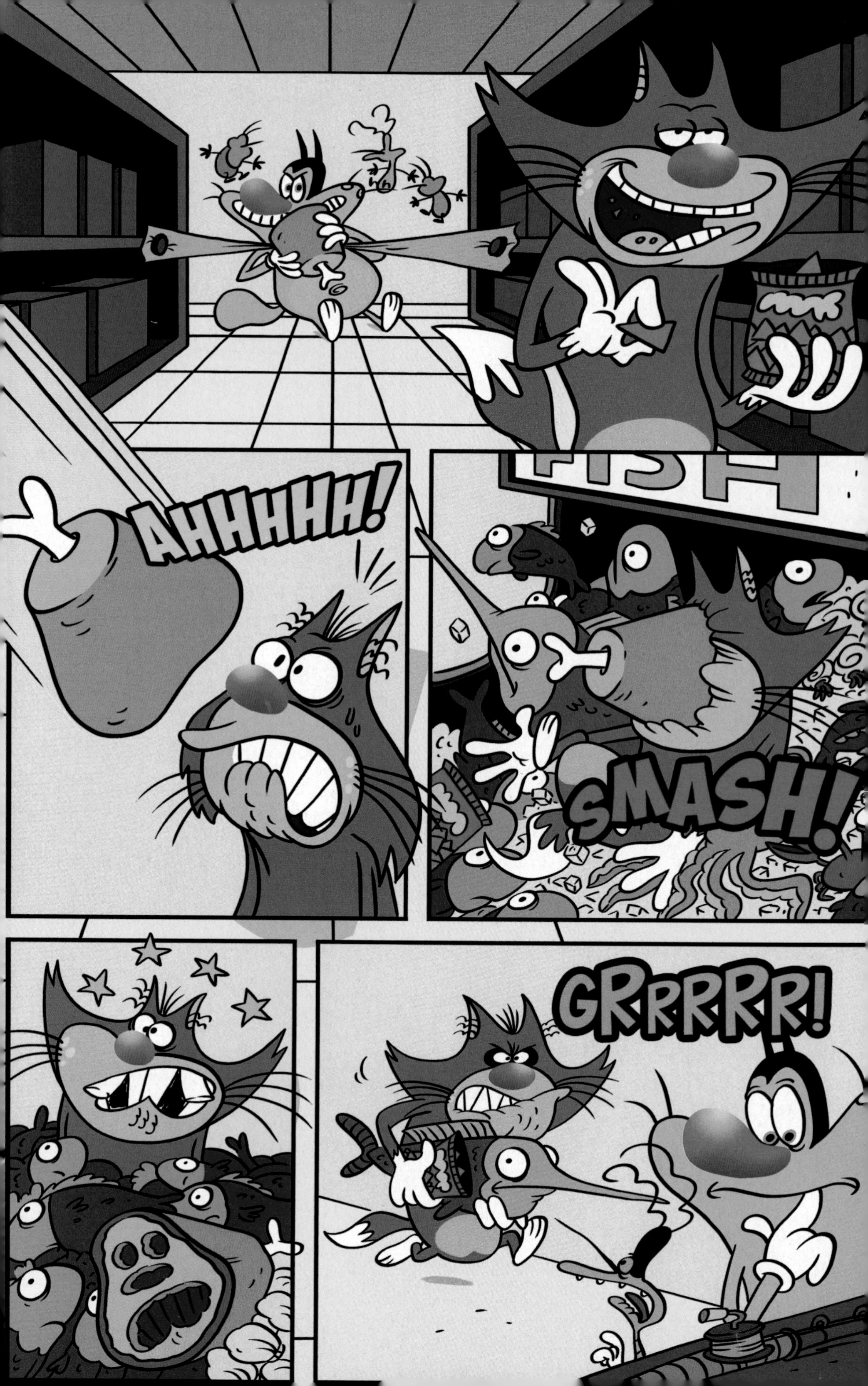
AHHHHHH!
FISH
SMASH!
GRRRRR!

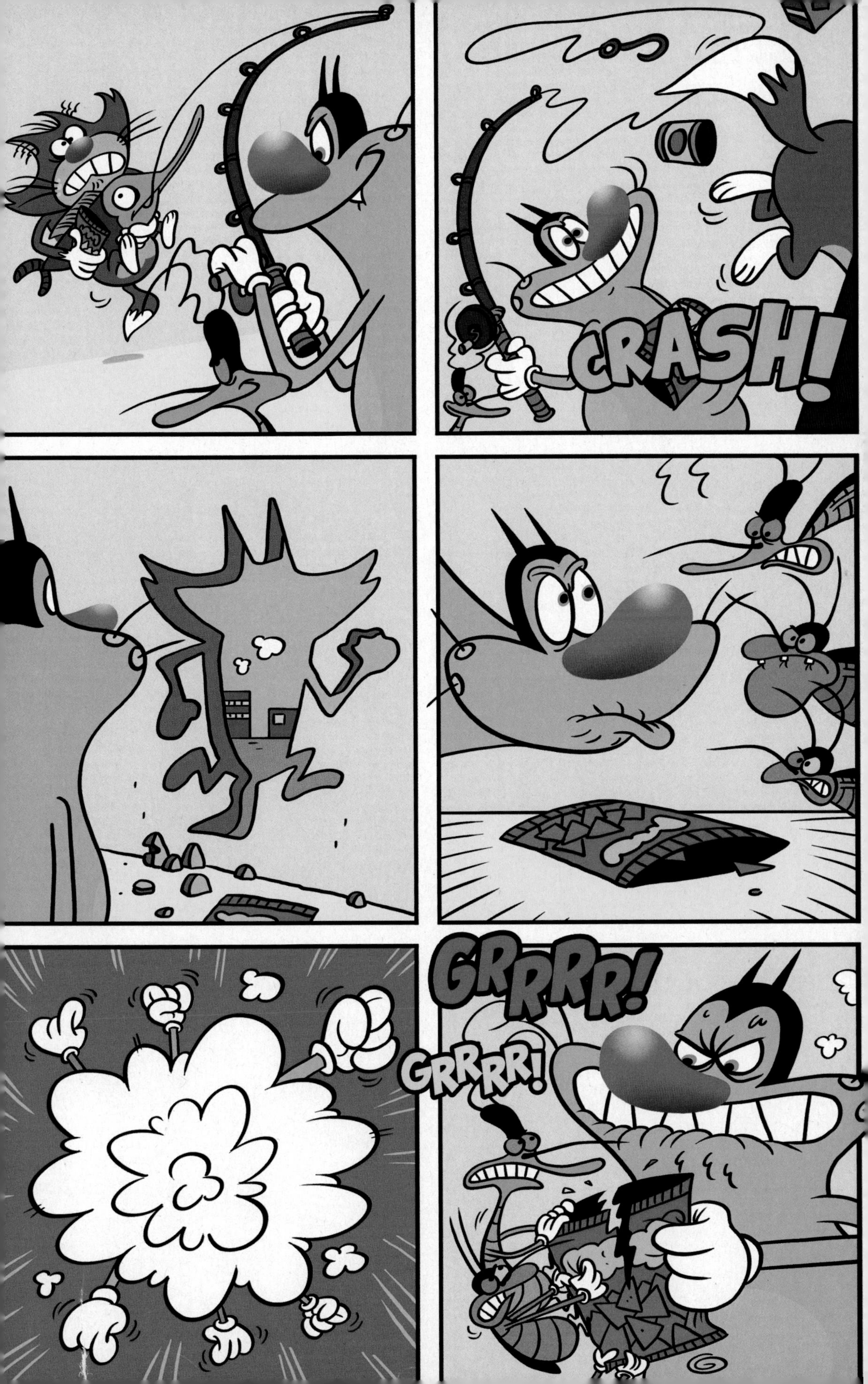
CRASH!
GRRRRR!
GRRRRR!

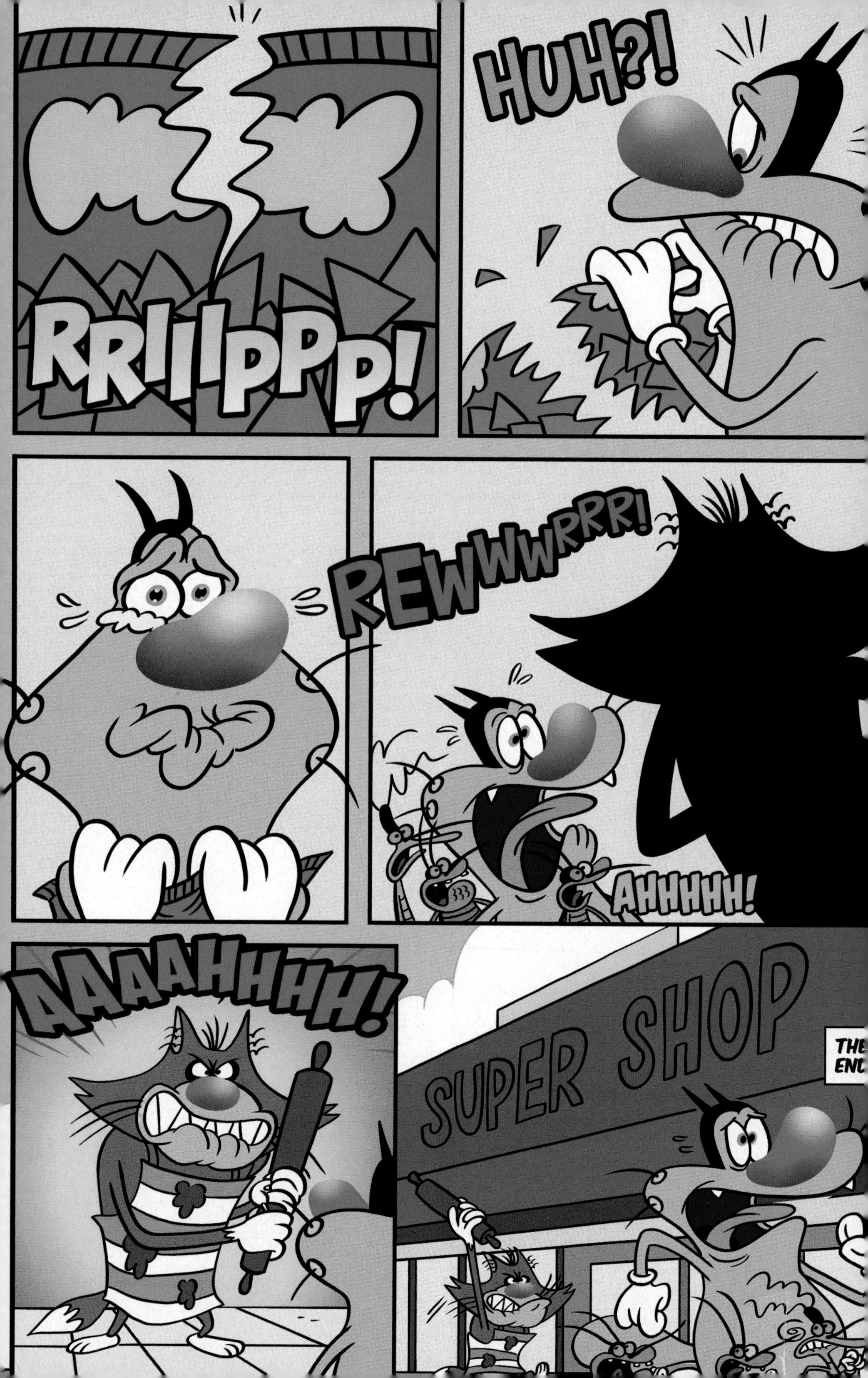
RRIIIPPPP!
HUH?!
REWWWRRR!
AHHHHH!
AAAAHHHHH!
SUPER SHOP
THE END

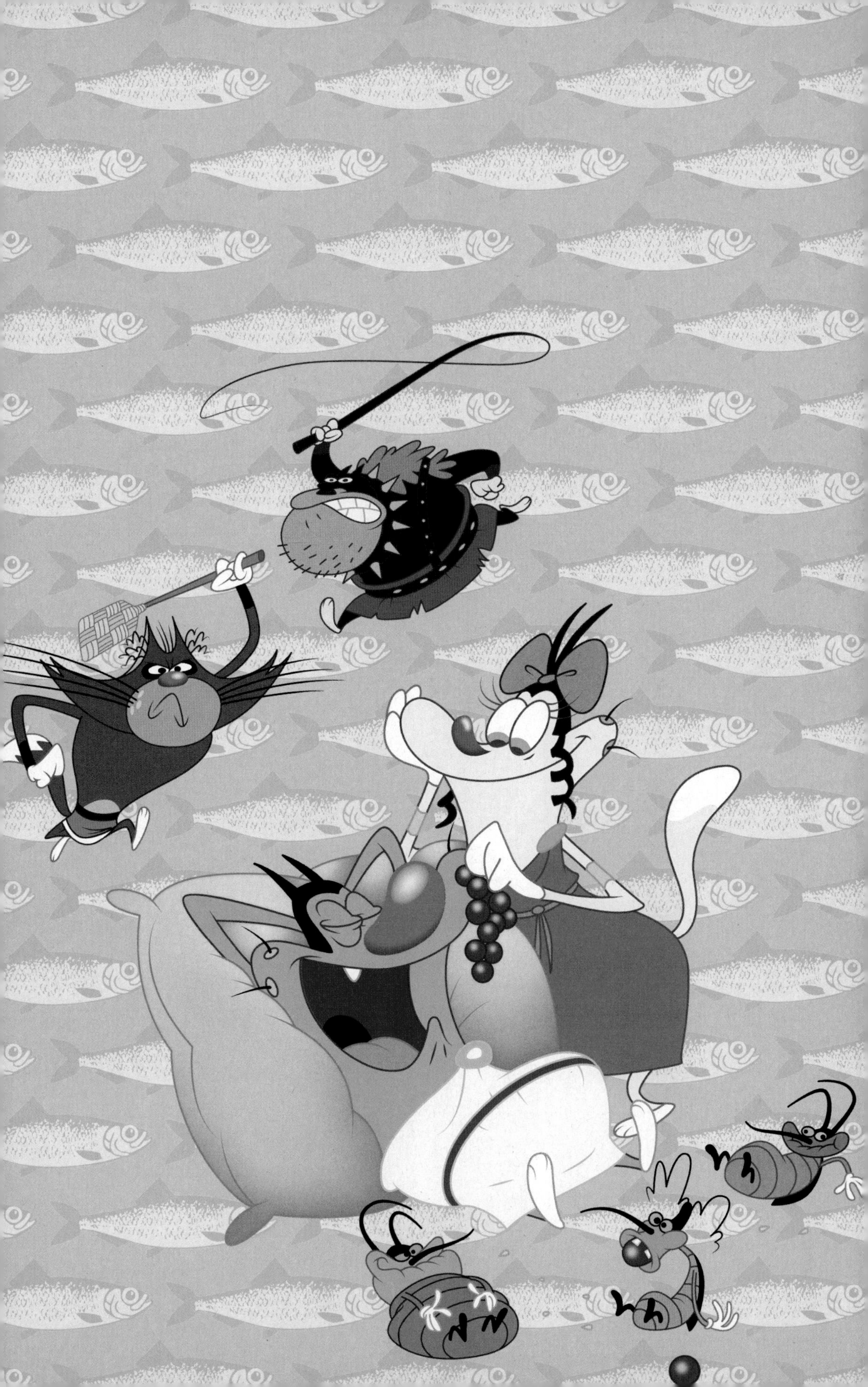

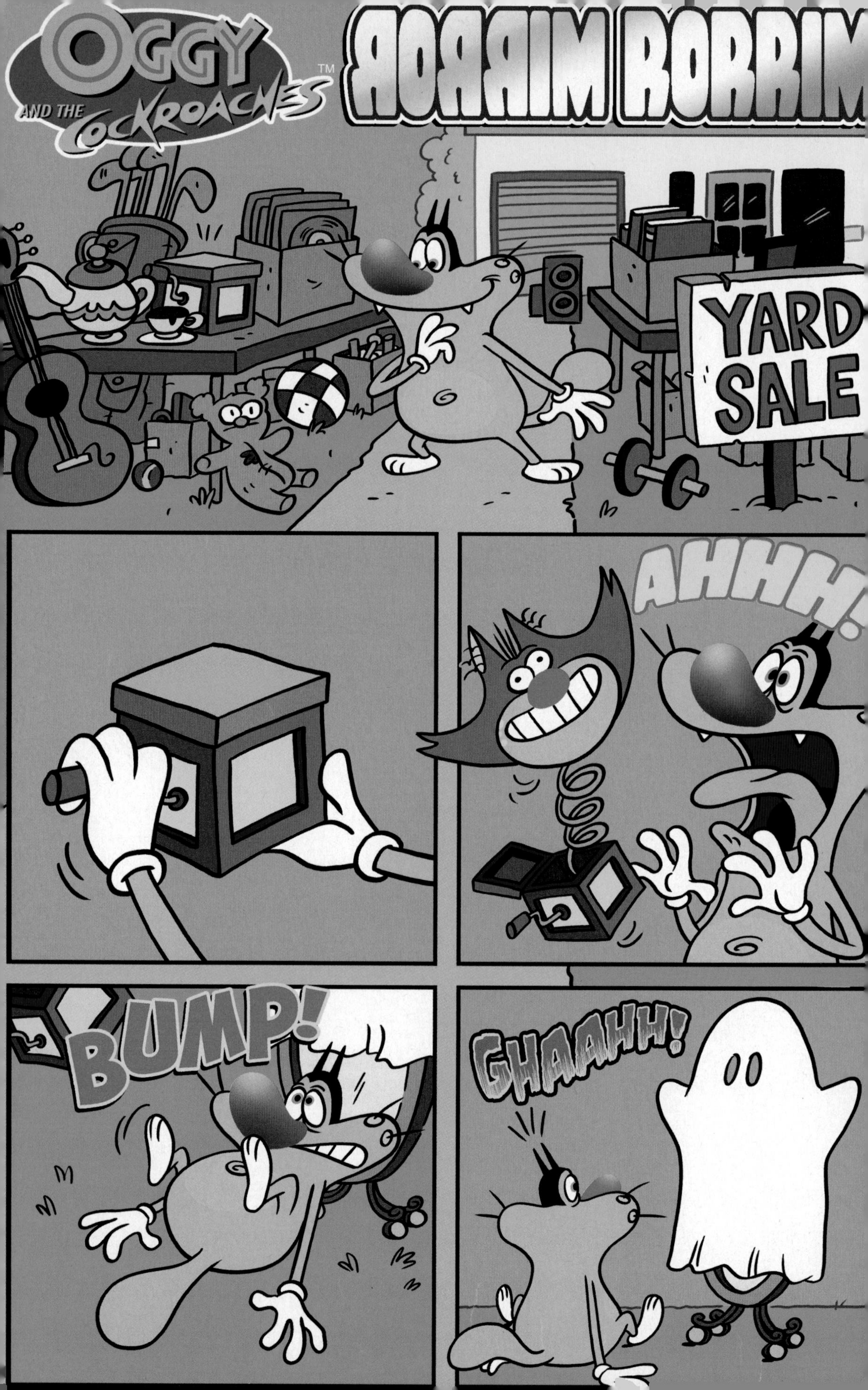
OGGY AND THE COCKROACHES ™
YARD SALE
AHHH!
BUMP!
GHAAHH!

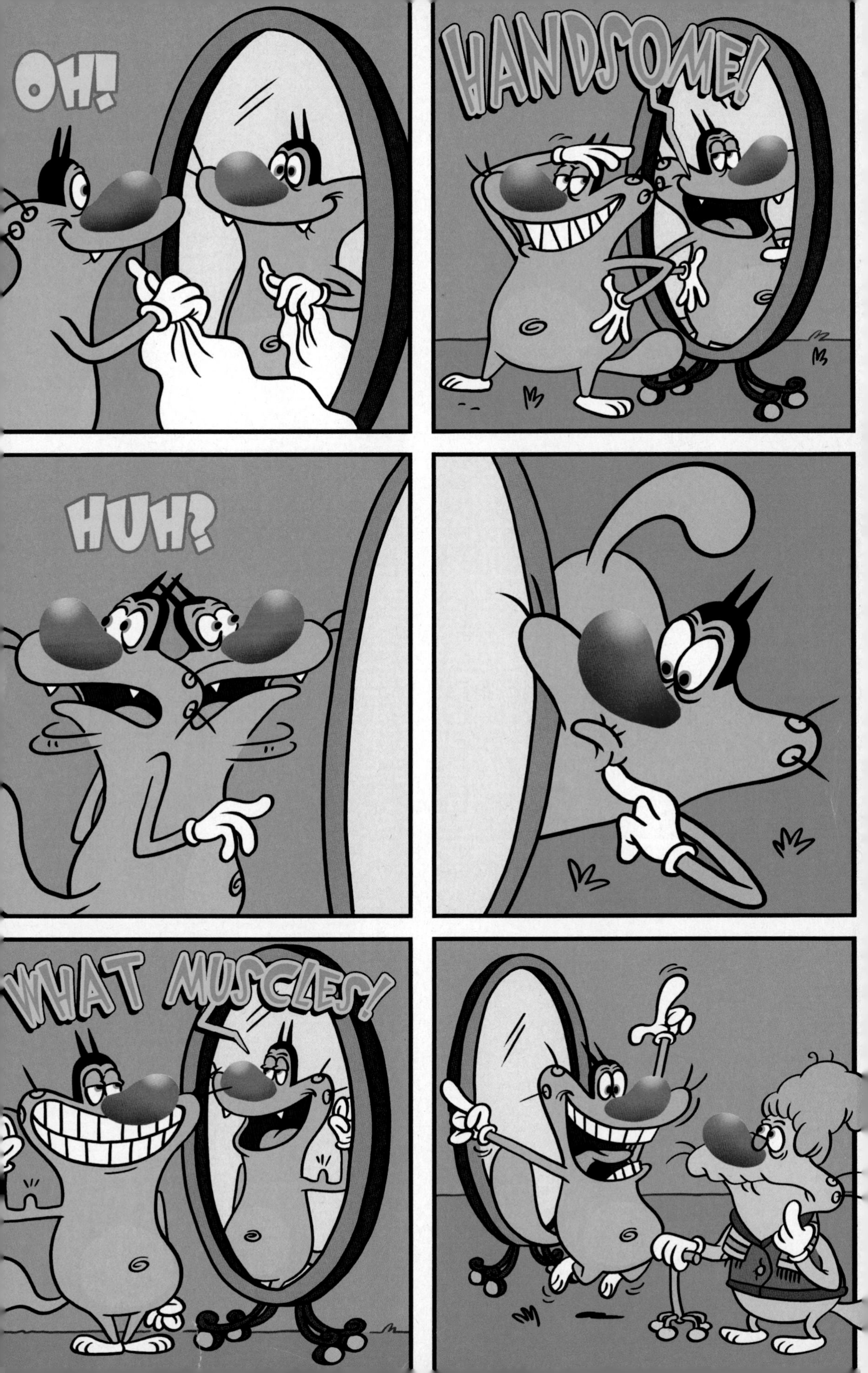
OH!
HANDSOME!
HUH?
WHAT MUSCLES!

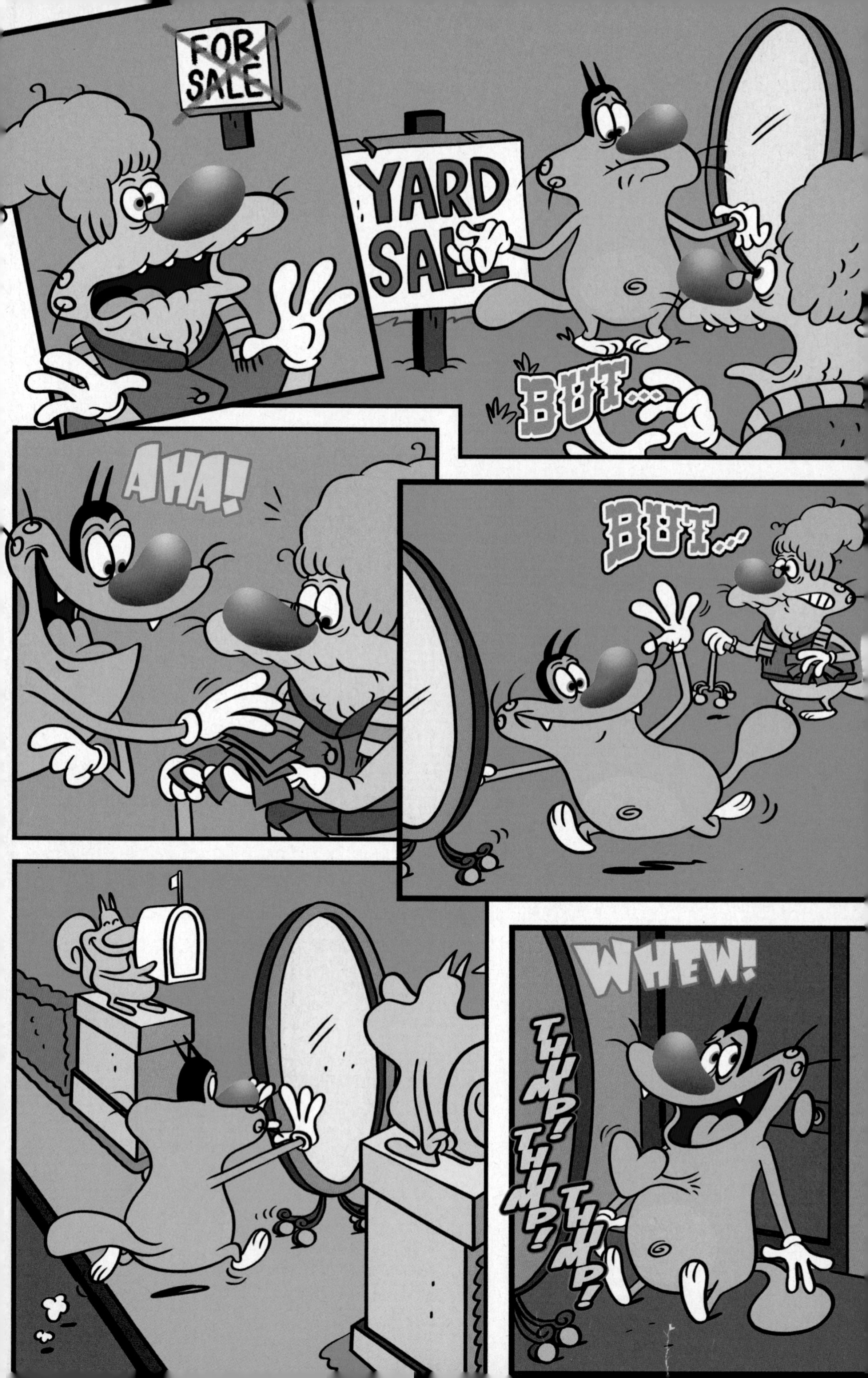
FOR SALE
YARD SALE
BUT...
AHA!
BUT...
WHEW!
THUMP! THUMP! THUMP! THUMP!

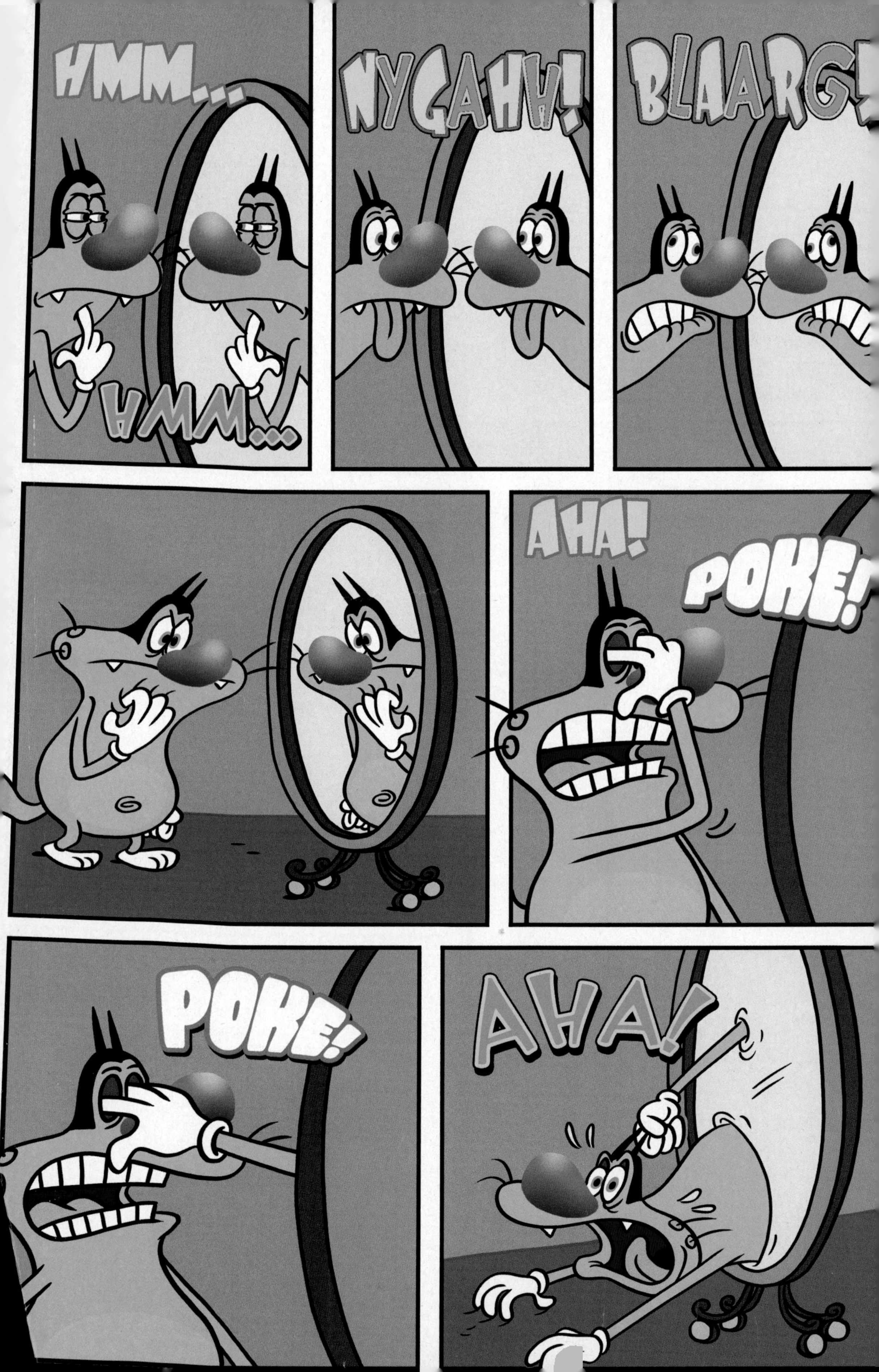
HMM...
HMM...
NYGAHH!
BLAARG!
AHA!
POKE!
POKE!
AHA!

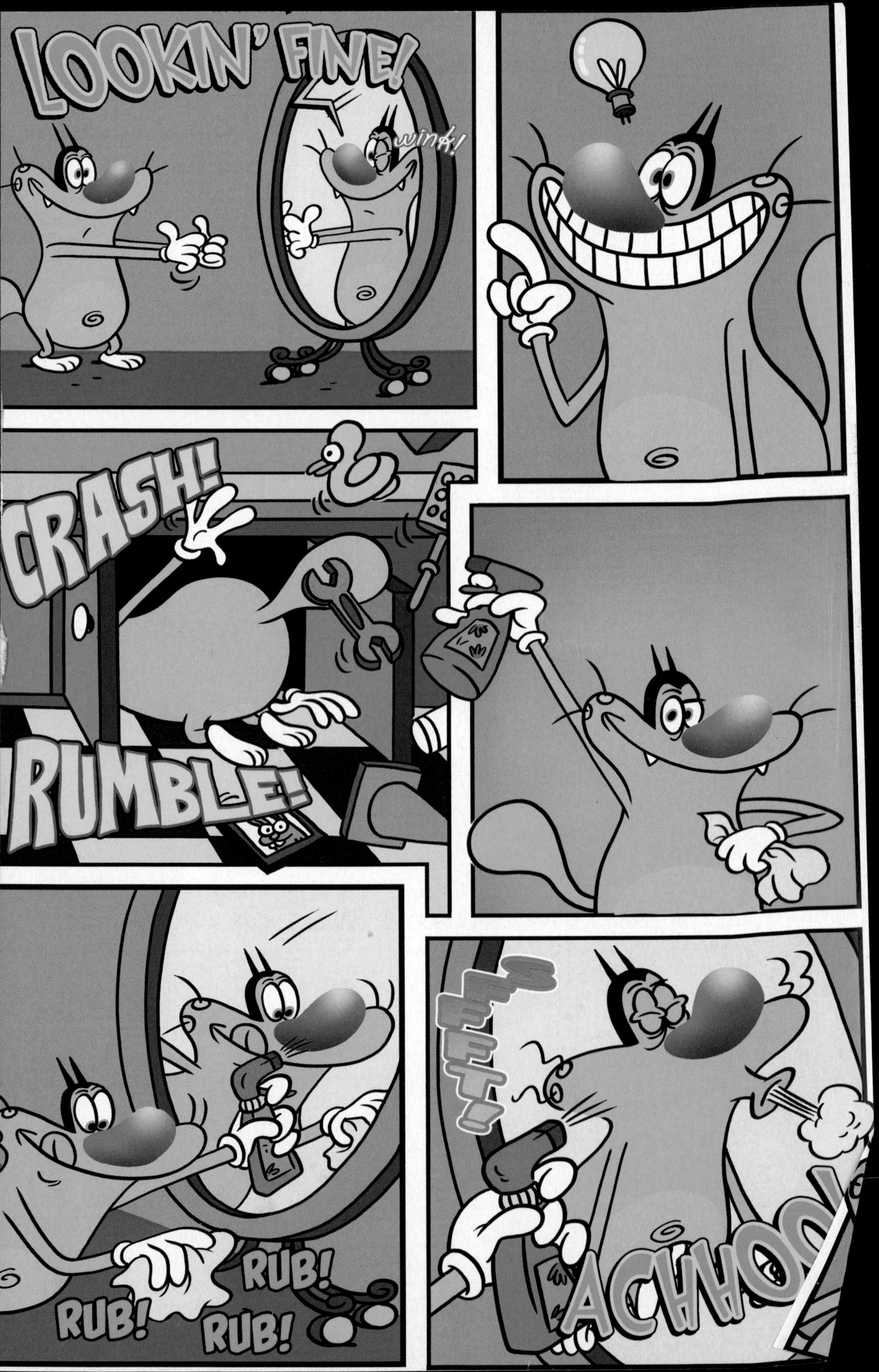

LOOKIN' FINE!
wink!
CRASH!
RUMBLE!
RUB!
RUB!
RUB!
SFFFT!
ACHOO!

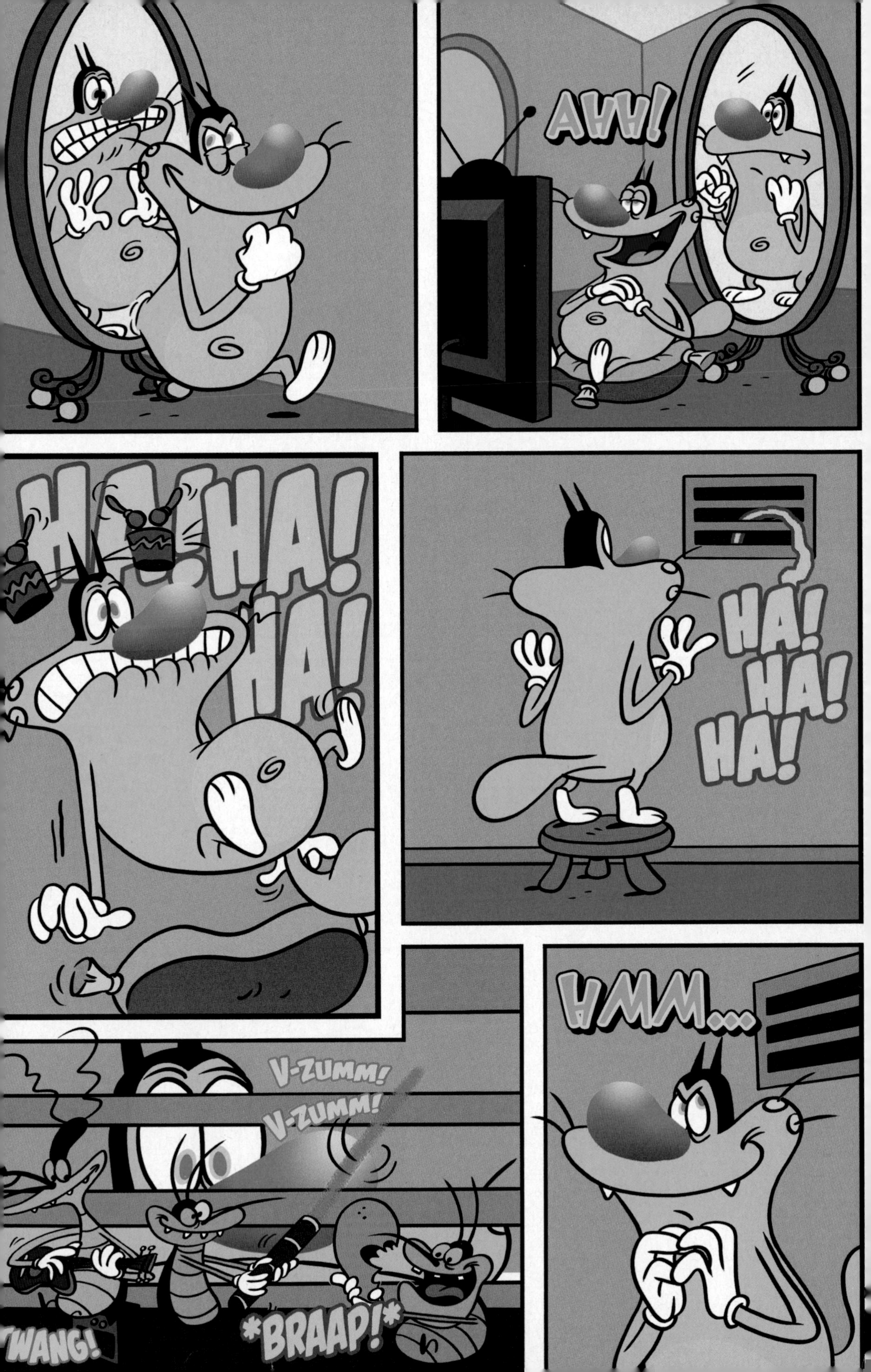
AHH!
HA!HA!
HA!
HA!
HA!
HA!
HMM...
V-ZUMM!
V-ZUMM!
TWANG!
BRAAP!

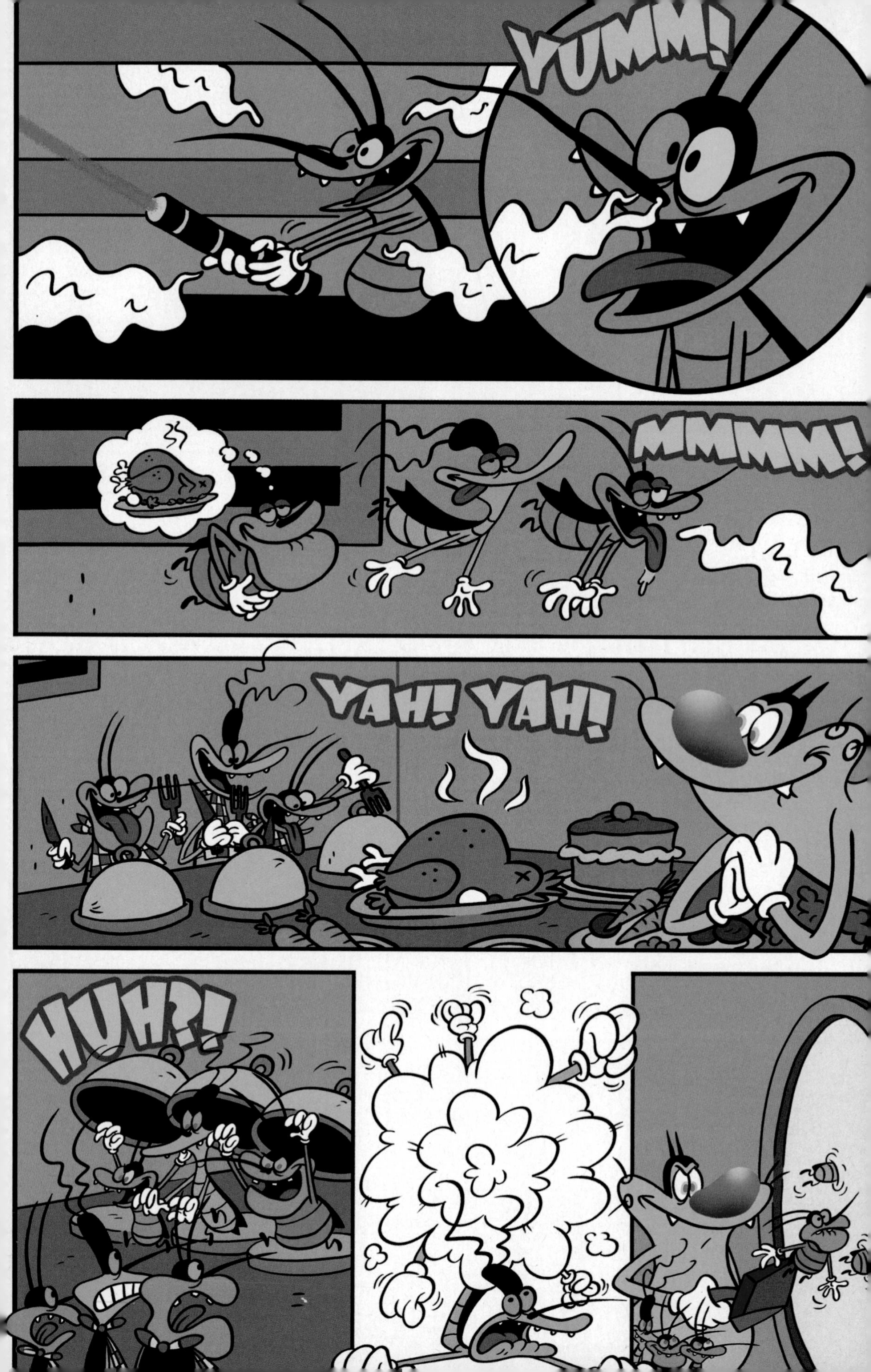
YUMM!
MMMMM!
YAH! YAH!
HUH?!

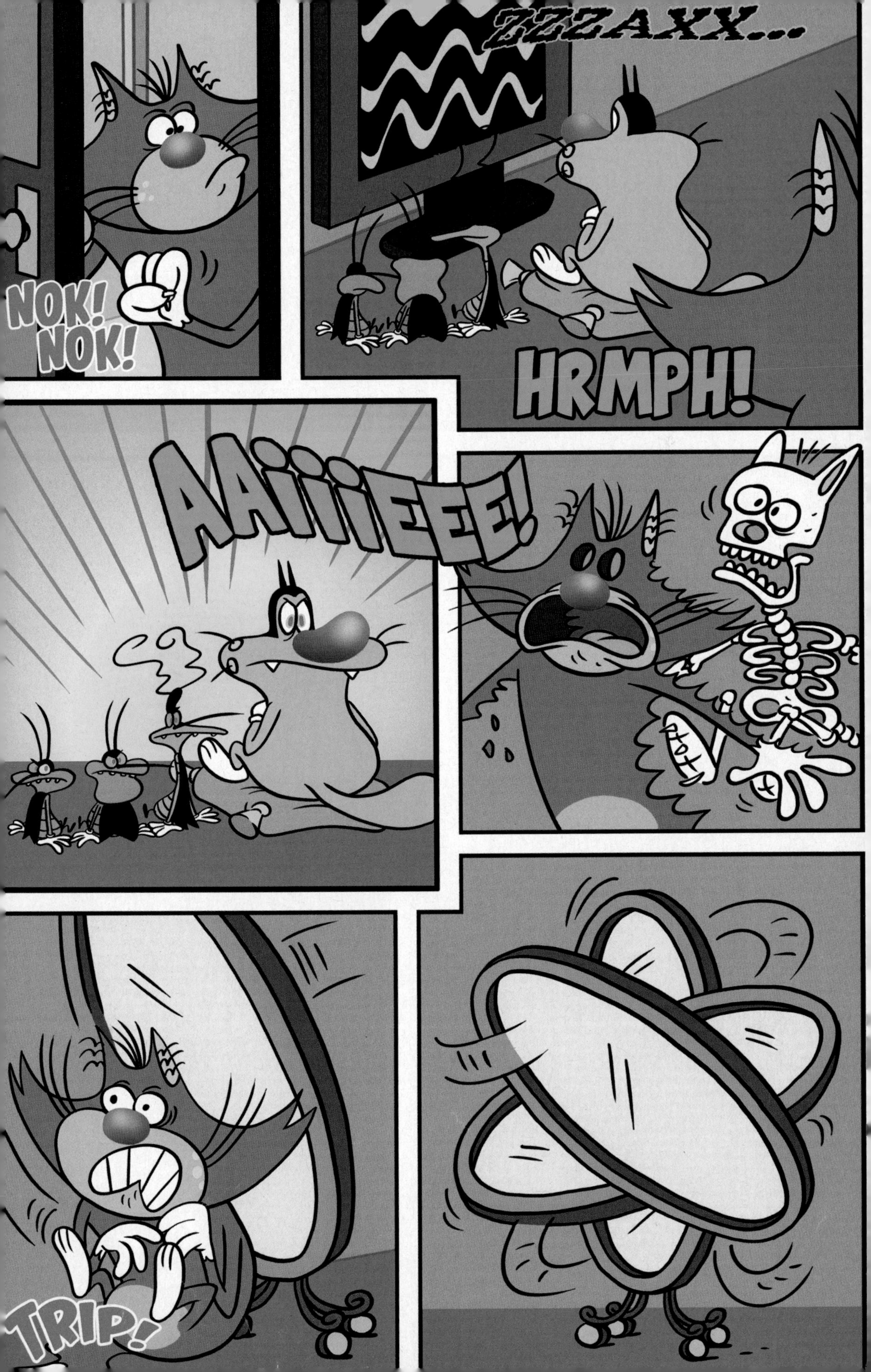
NOK! NOK!
ZZZAXX...
HRMPH!
AAiiiiEEE!
TRIP!

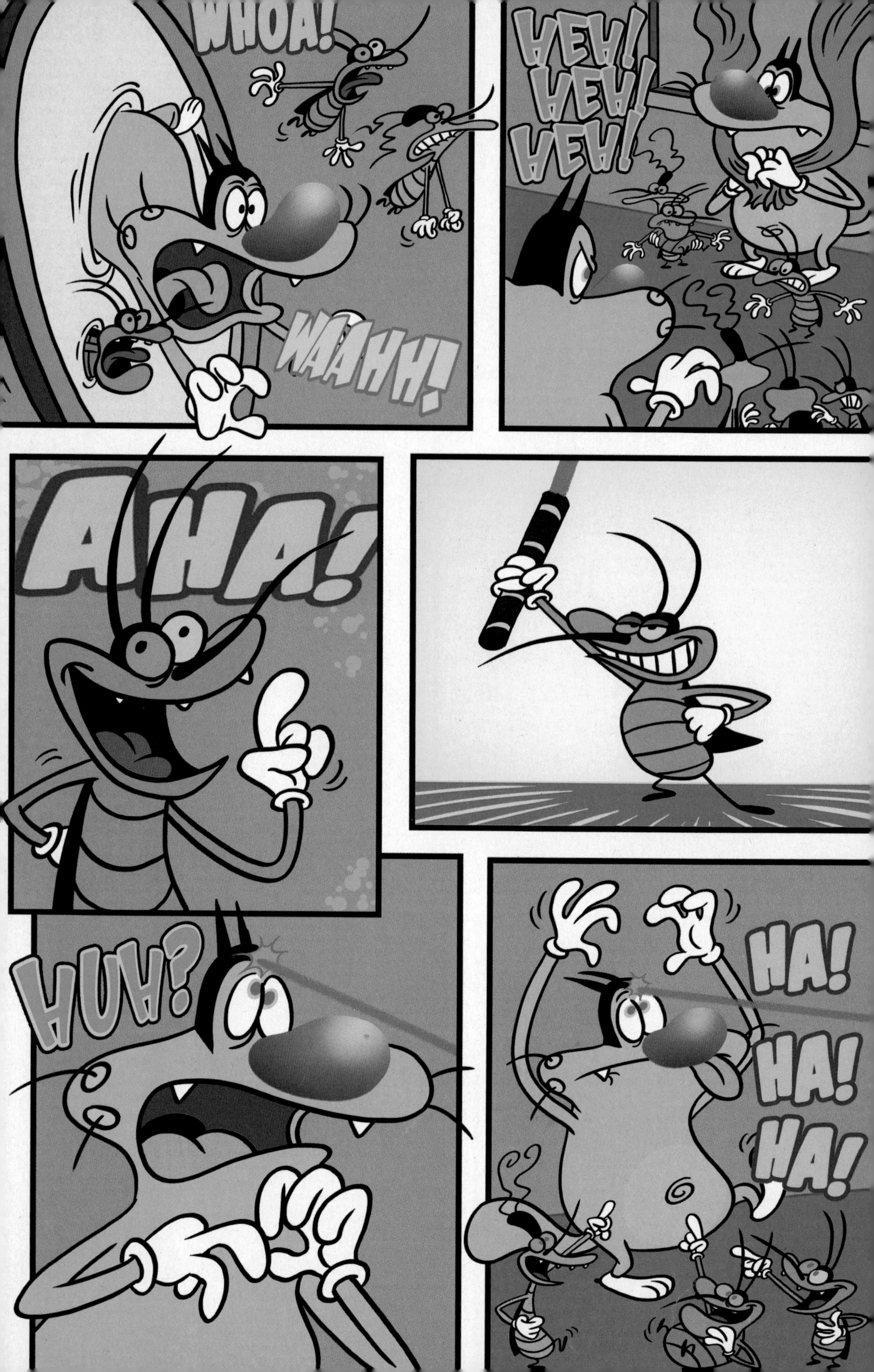
WHOA!
WAAHH!
HEH! HEH! HEH!
AHA!
HUH?
HA! HA! HA!

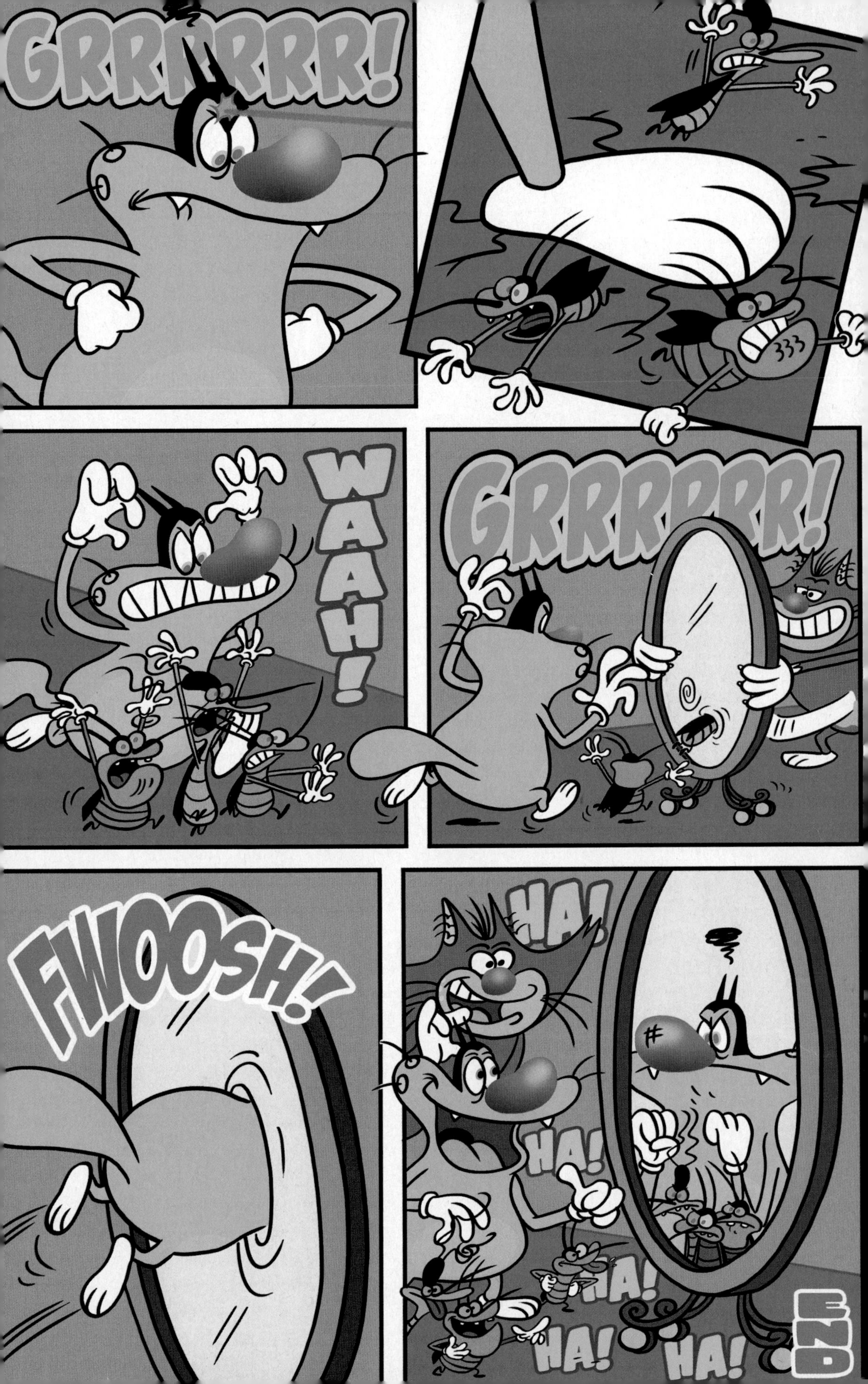
GRRRRRRR!
WAAH!
GRRRRRR!
FWOOSH!
HA!
HA!
HA!
HA!
HA!
END

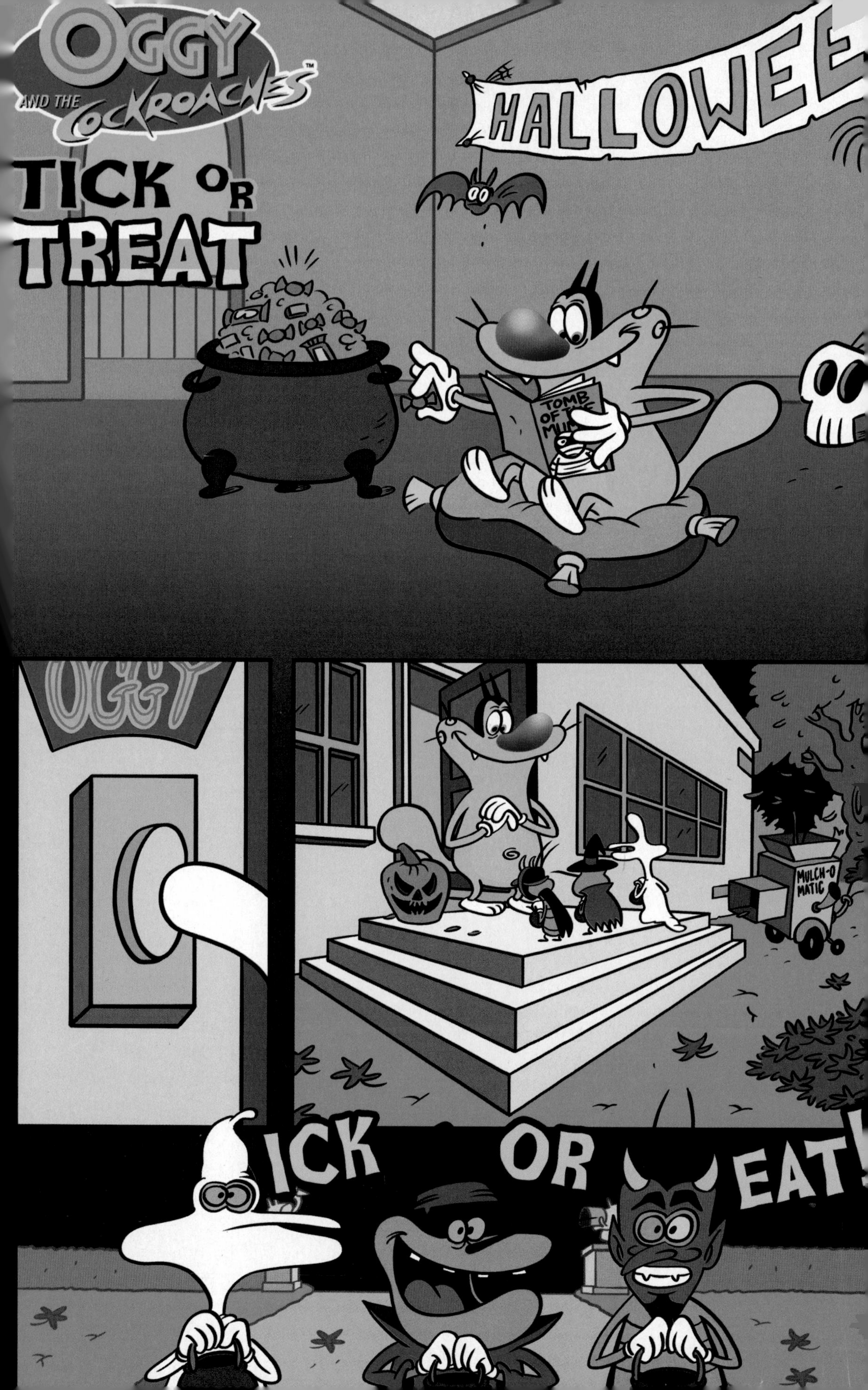
OGGY AND THE COCKROACHES™
TICK OR TREAT
HALLOWEE
TOMB
OGGY
MULCH-O MATIC
ICK OR EAT!

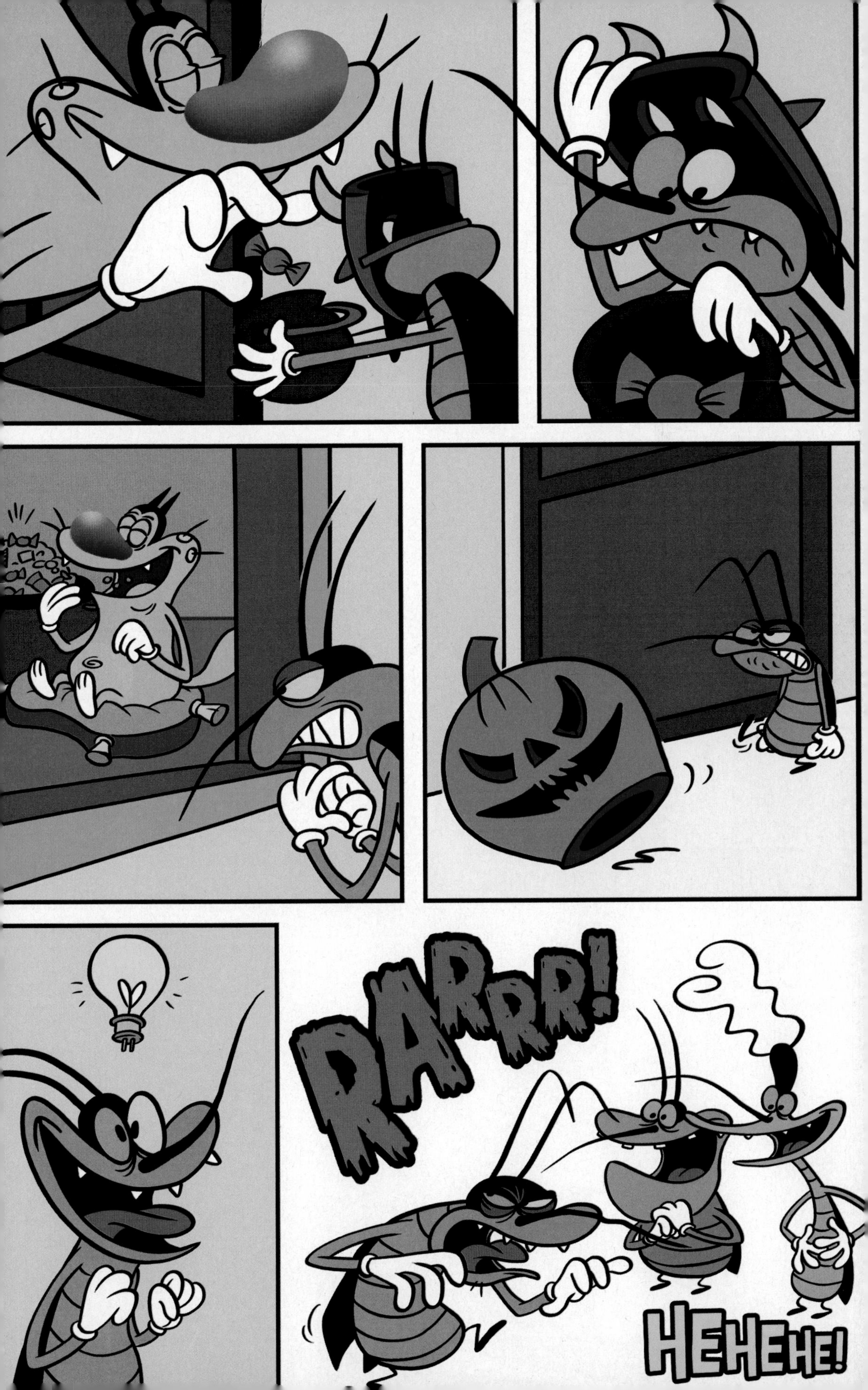
RARRR!
HEHEHE!

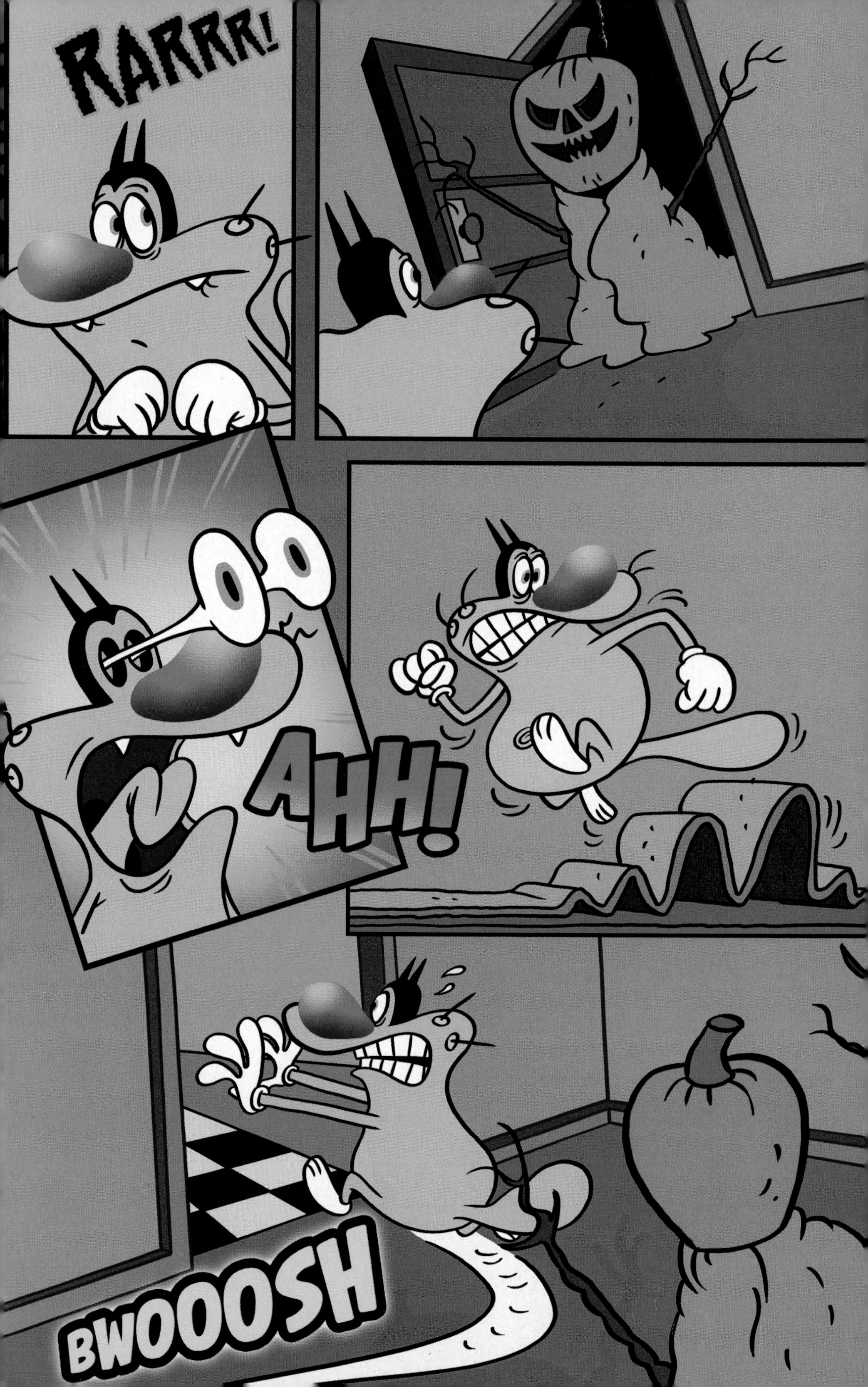
RARRR!
AHH!
BWOOOSH

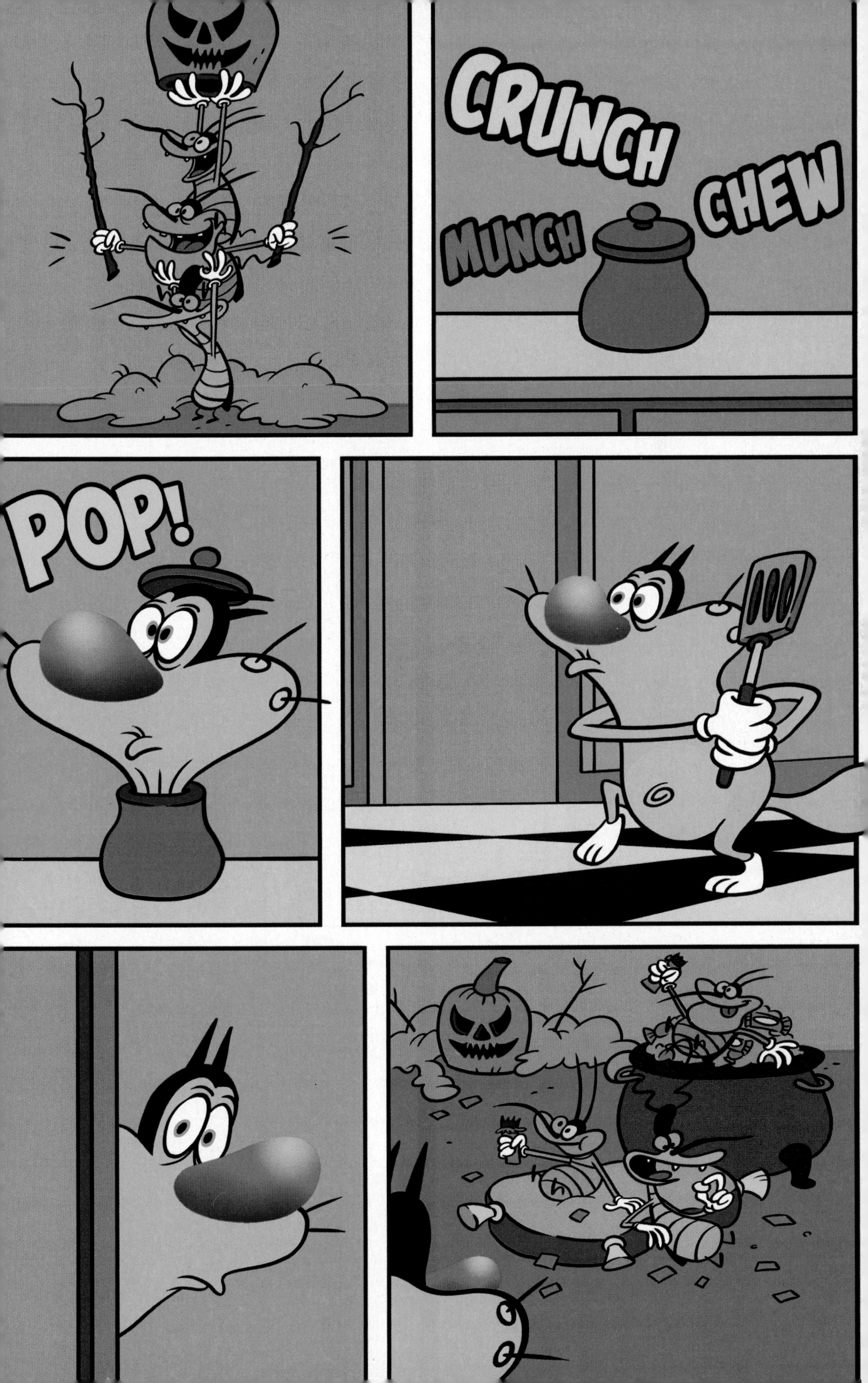
CRUNCH
MUNCH
CHEW
POP!

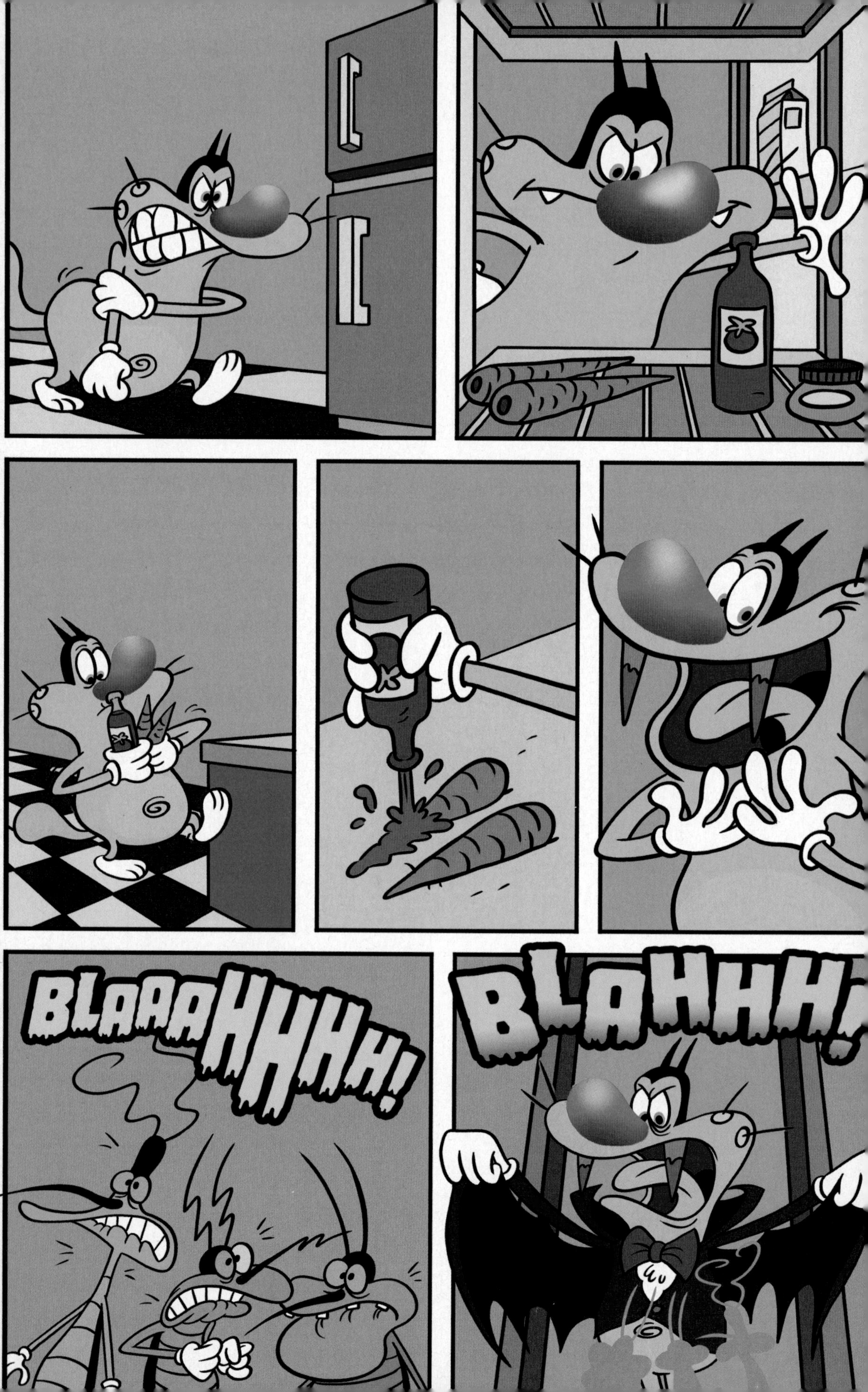
BLAAAHHHHH!
BLAHHHH!

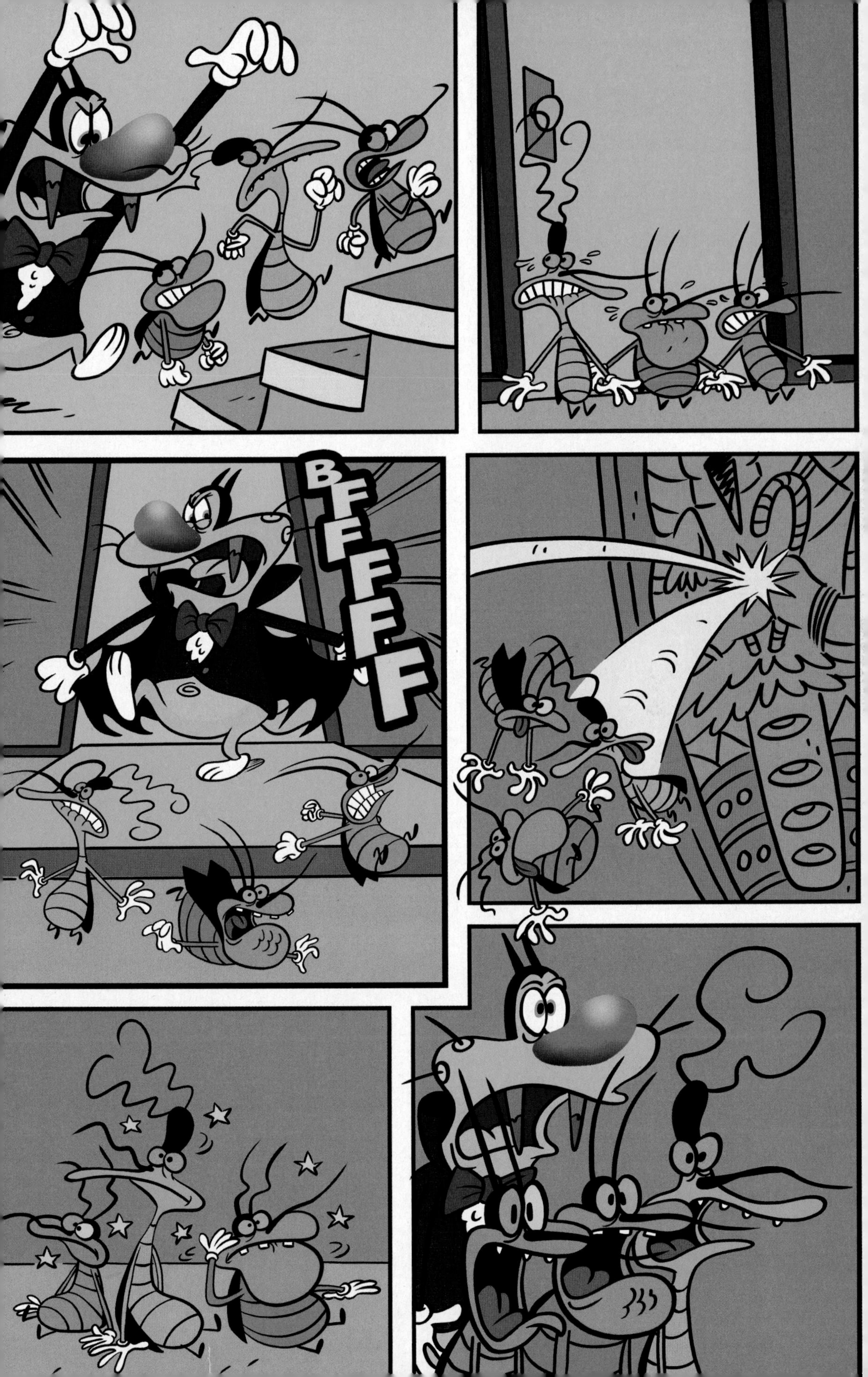
BFFFFF

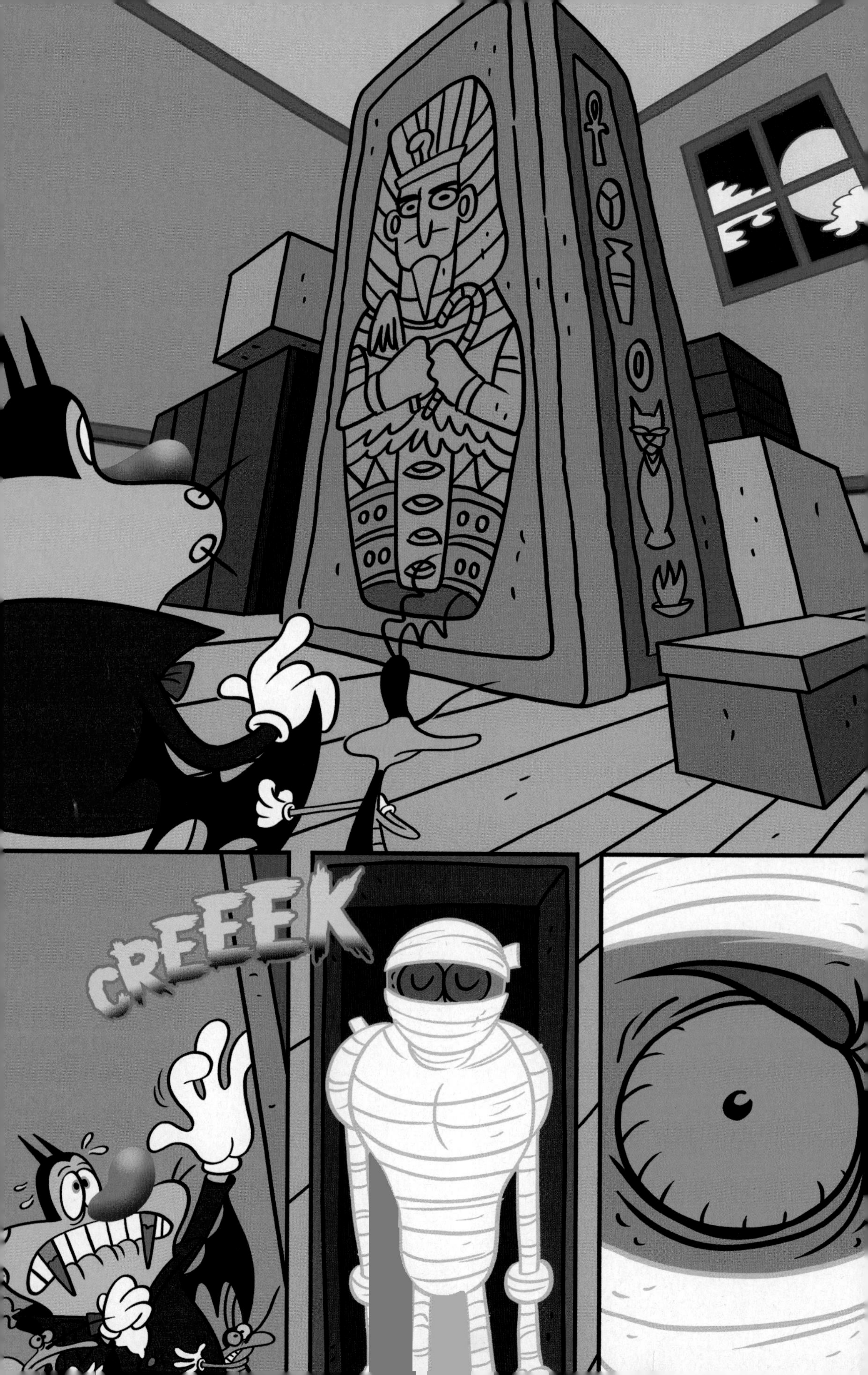
CREEEK

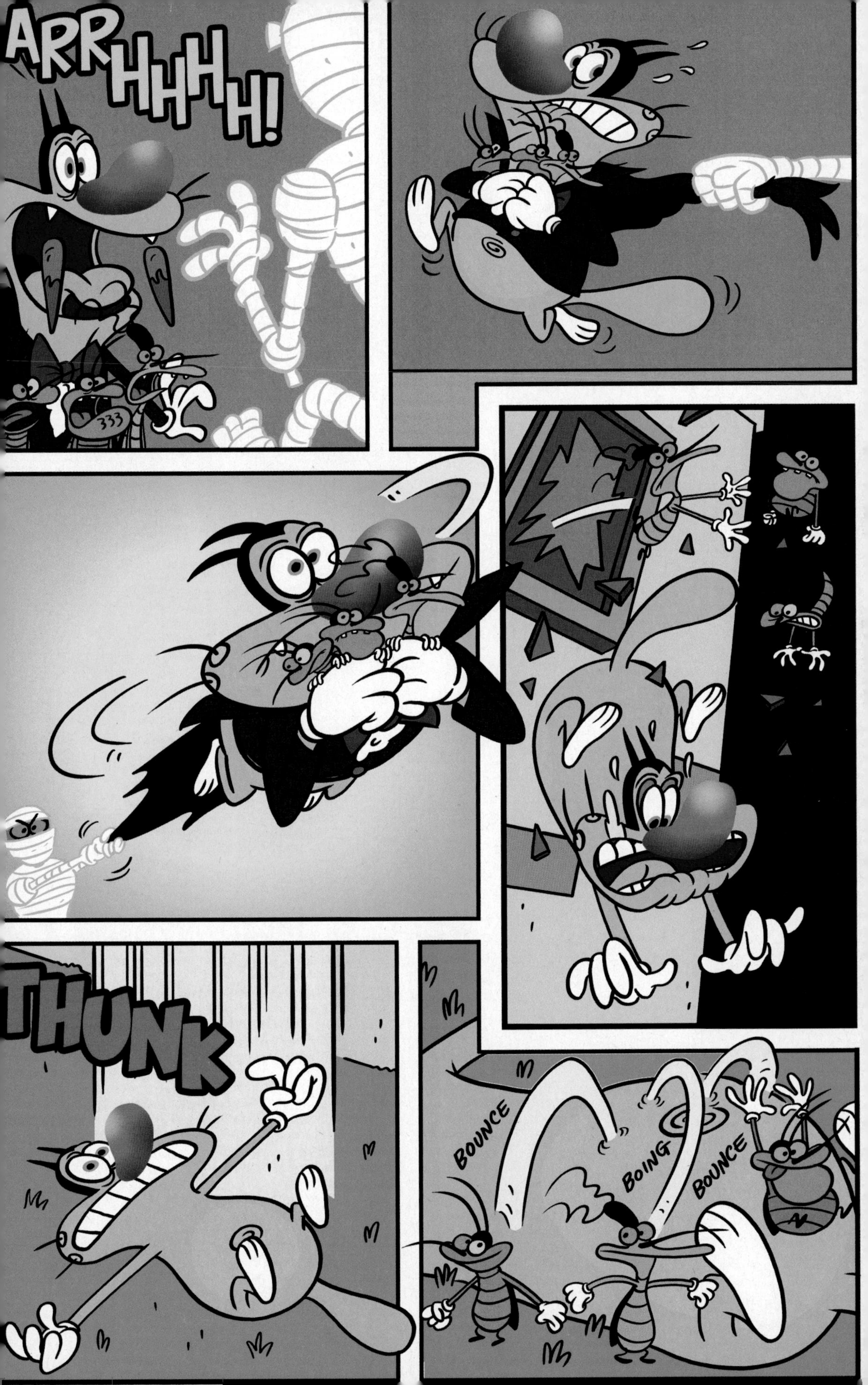
ARRHHHHH!
THUNK
BOUNCE
BOING
BOUNCE

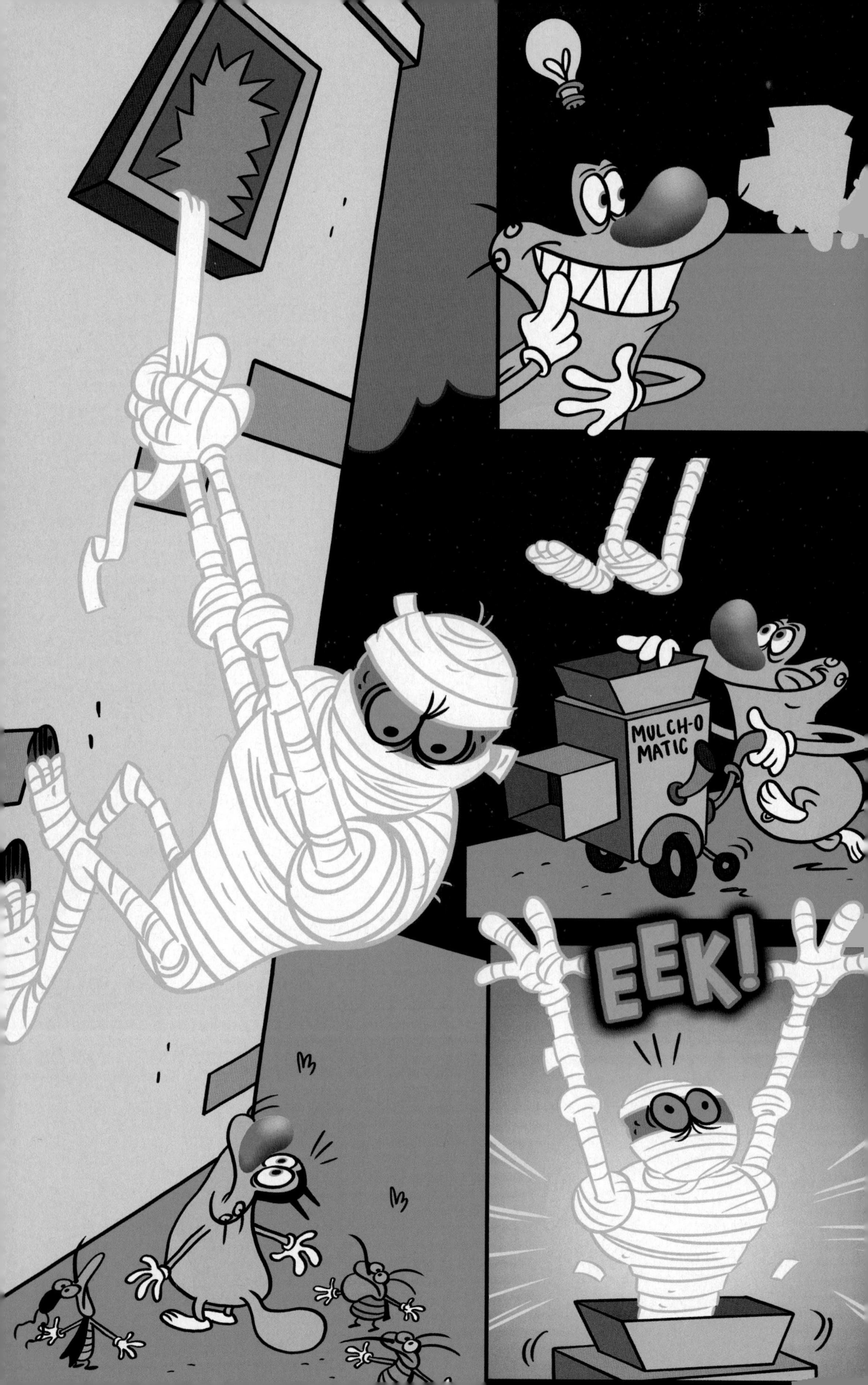
MULCH-O
MATIC
EEK!

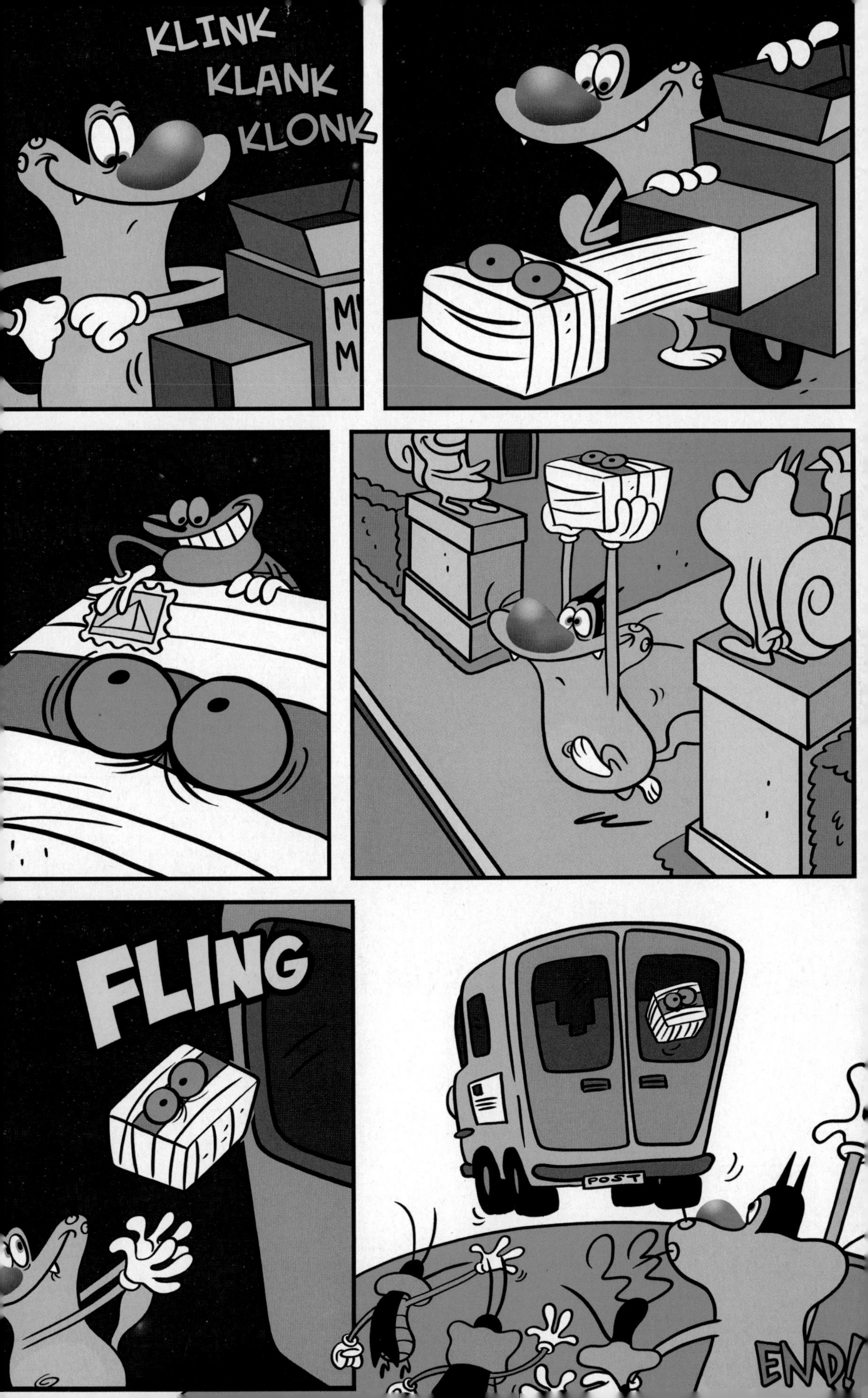
KLINK
KLANK
KLONK
FLING
POST
END!

BEHIND THE SCENES WITH ARTIST DEAN RANKINE

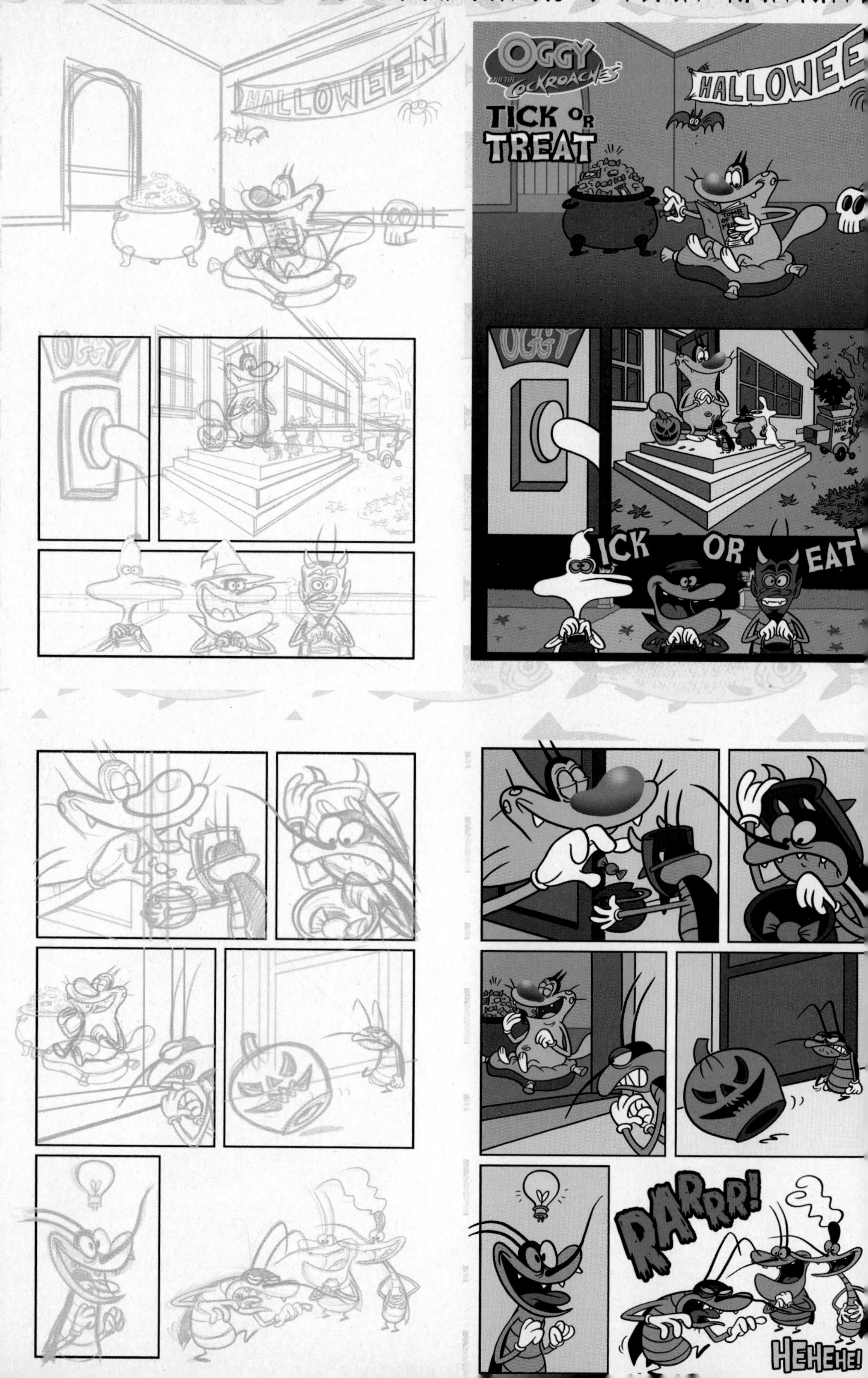

HALLOWEEN
OGGY AND THE COCKROACHES
TICK OR TREAT
HALLOWEE
OGGY
ICK
OR
EAT
RARRR!
HEHEHE!

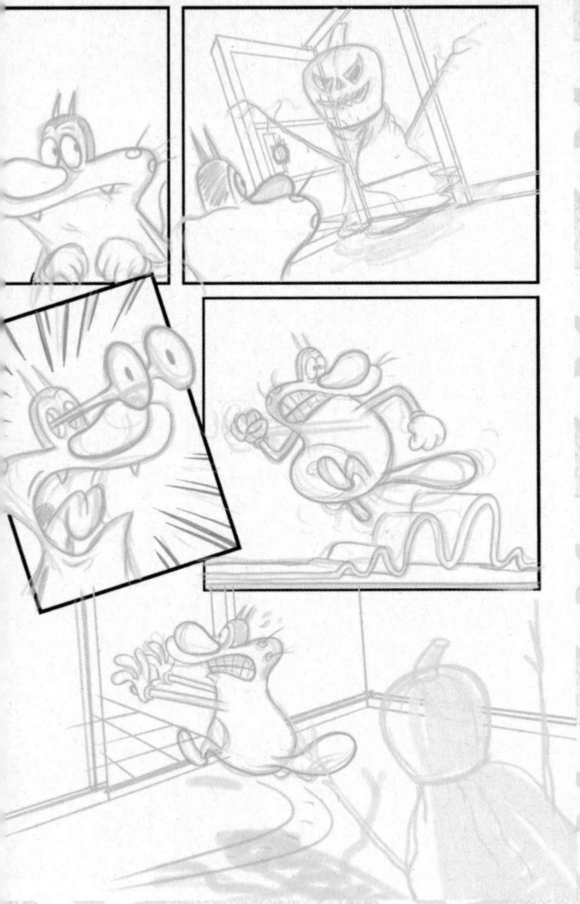

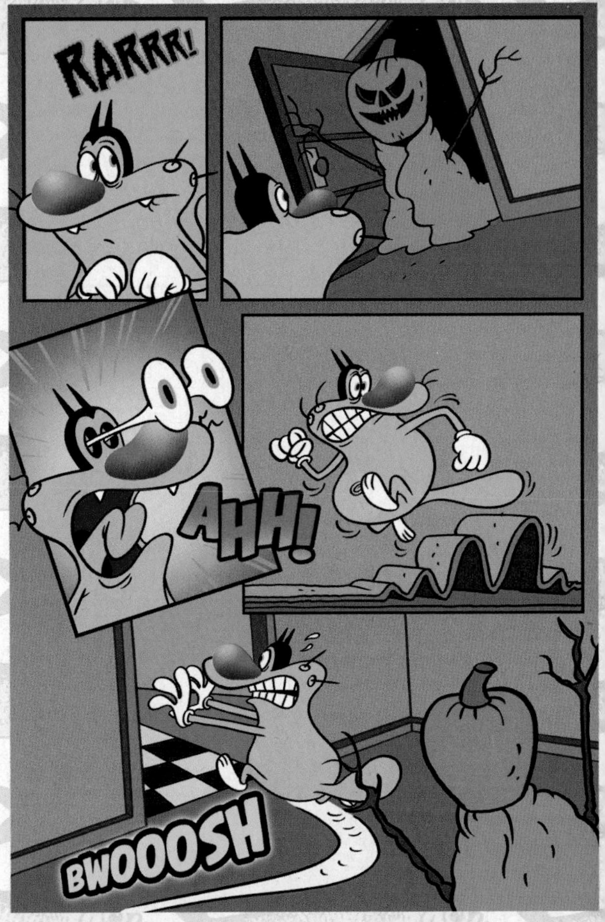
RARRR!
AHH!
BWOOOSH

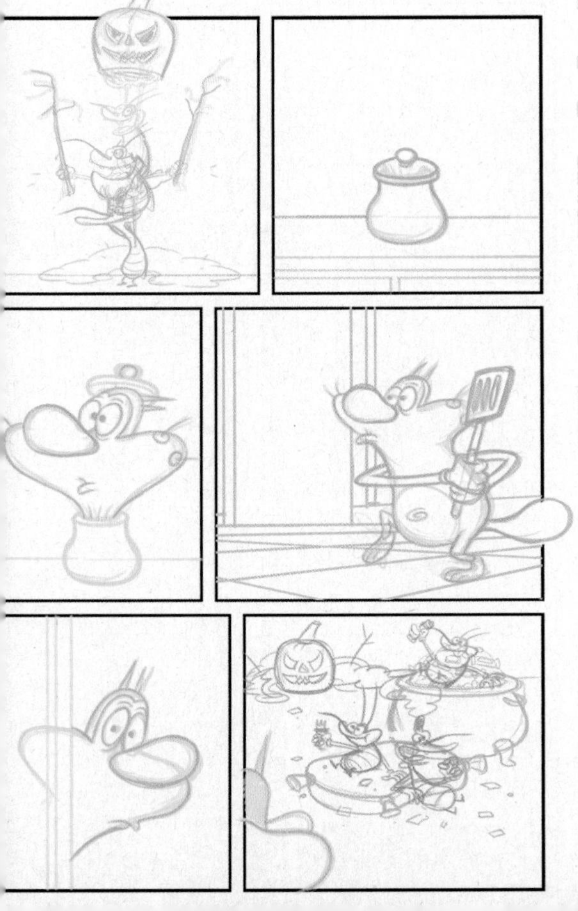

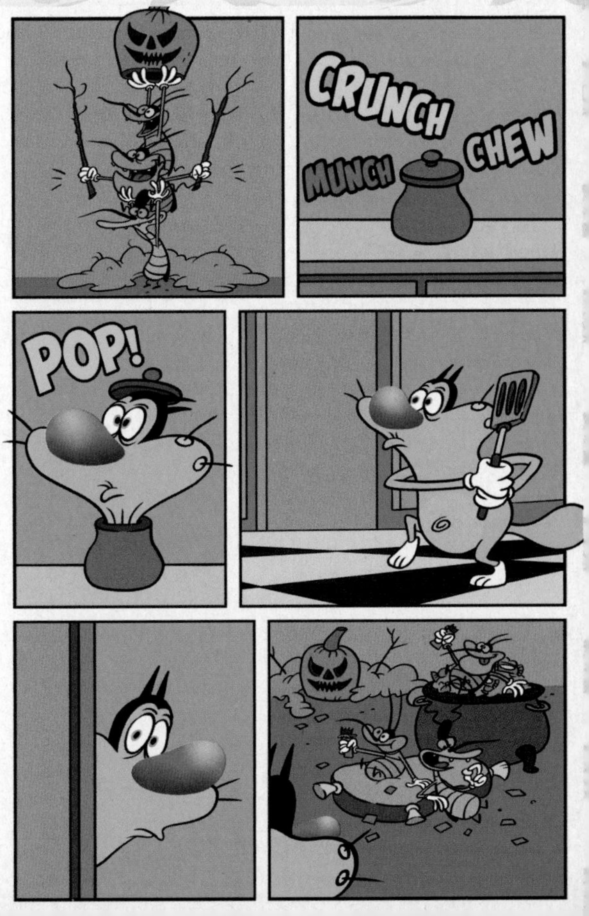
CRUNCH
MUNCH
CHEW
POP!

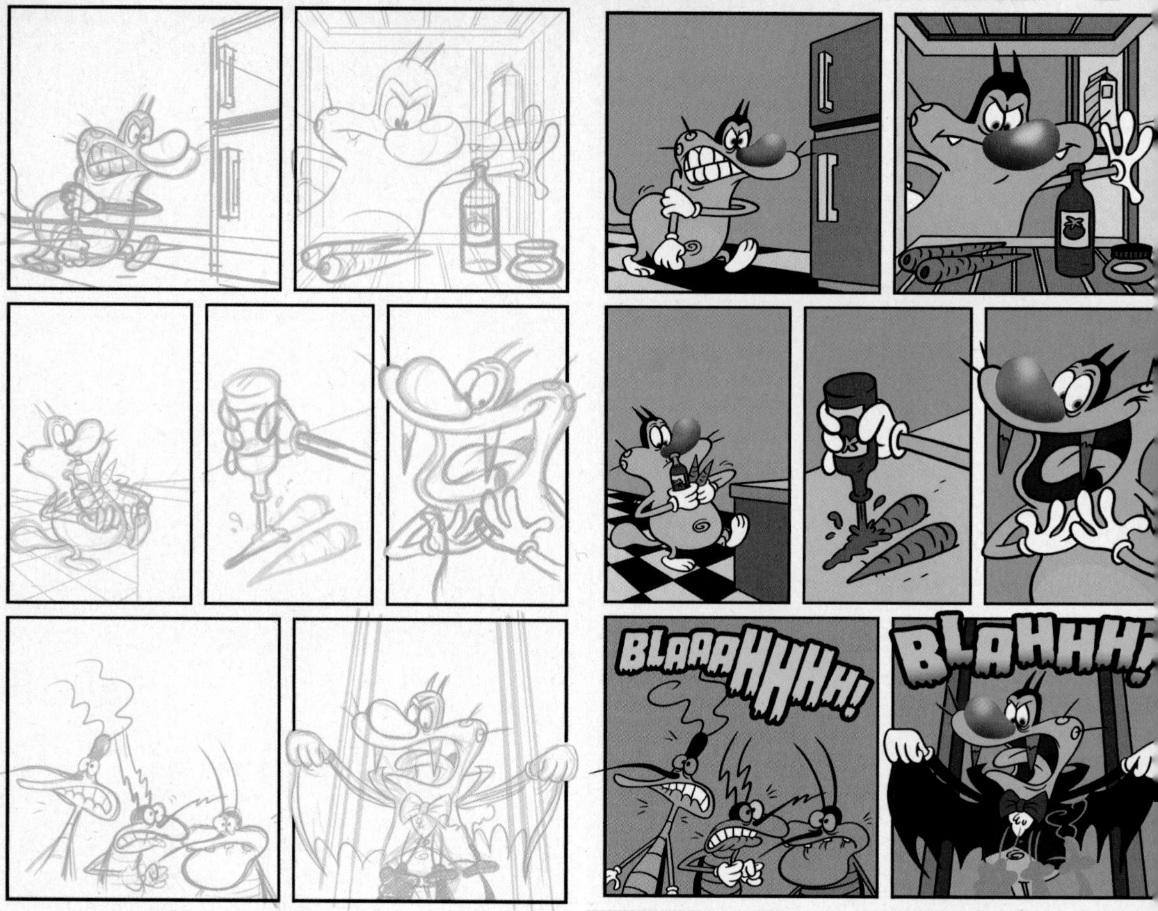
BLAAAHHHH!
BLAHHH!

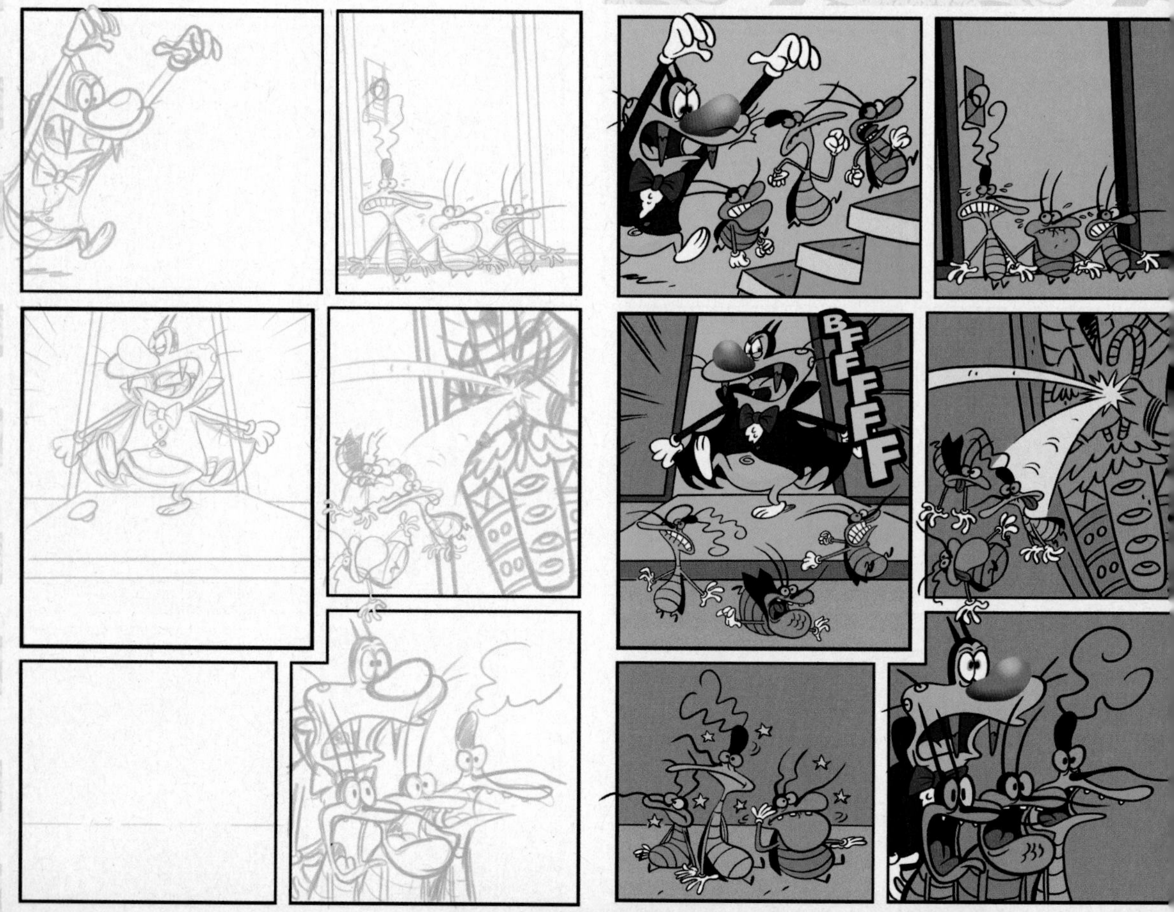
BFFFFF

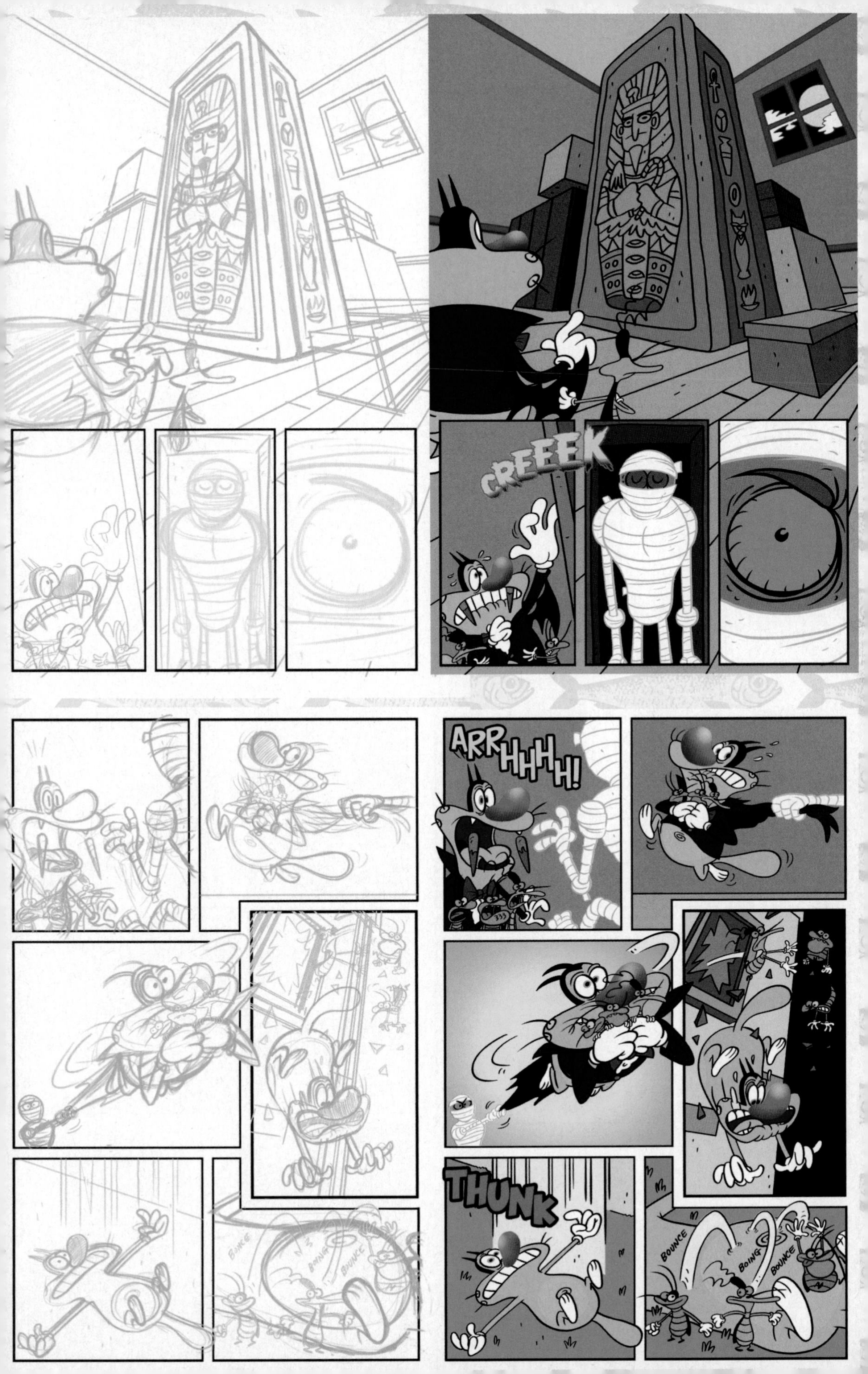

CREEEK
BOUNCE
BOING
BOUNCE
ARRHHHH!
THUNK
BOUNCE
BOING
BOUNCE

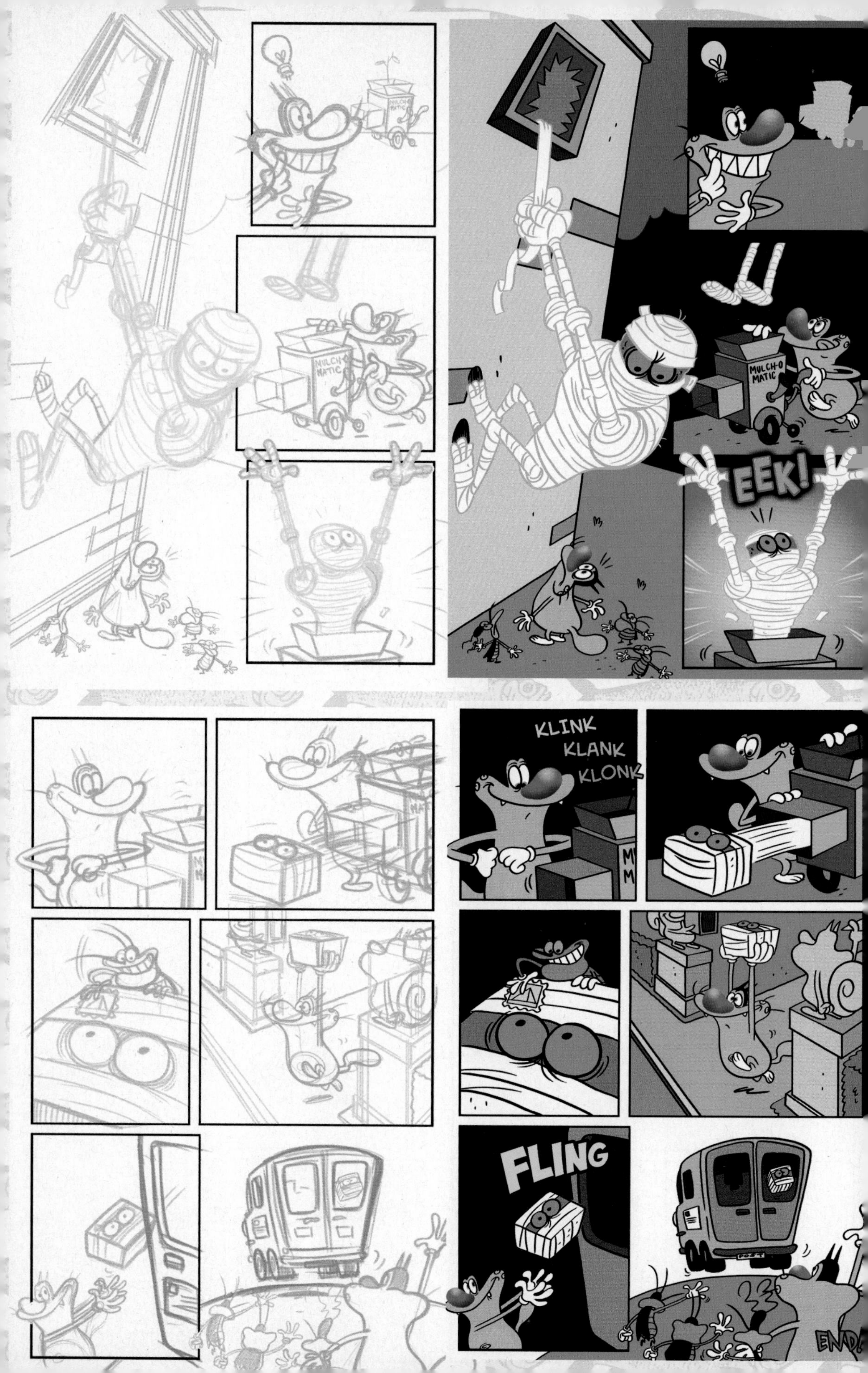
MULCH-O MATIC
MULCH-O MATIC
MULCH-O MATIC
EEK!
KLINK
KLANK
KLONK
FLING
END!

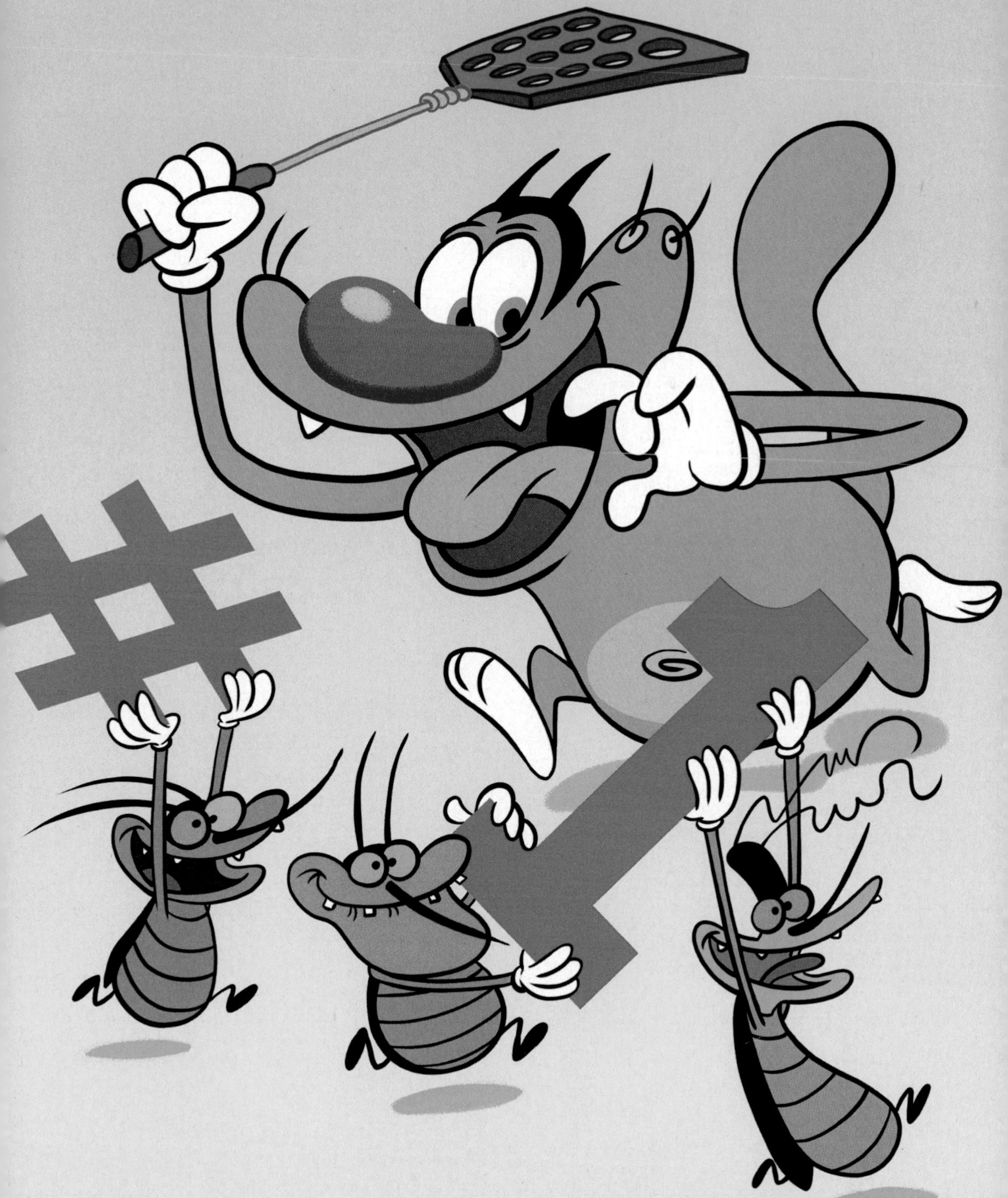

Cover art by Dean Rankine

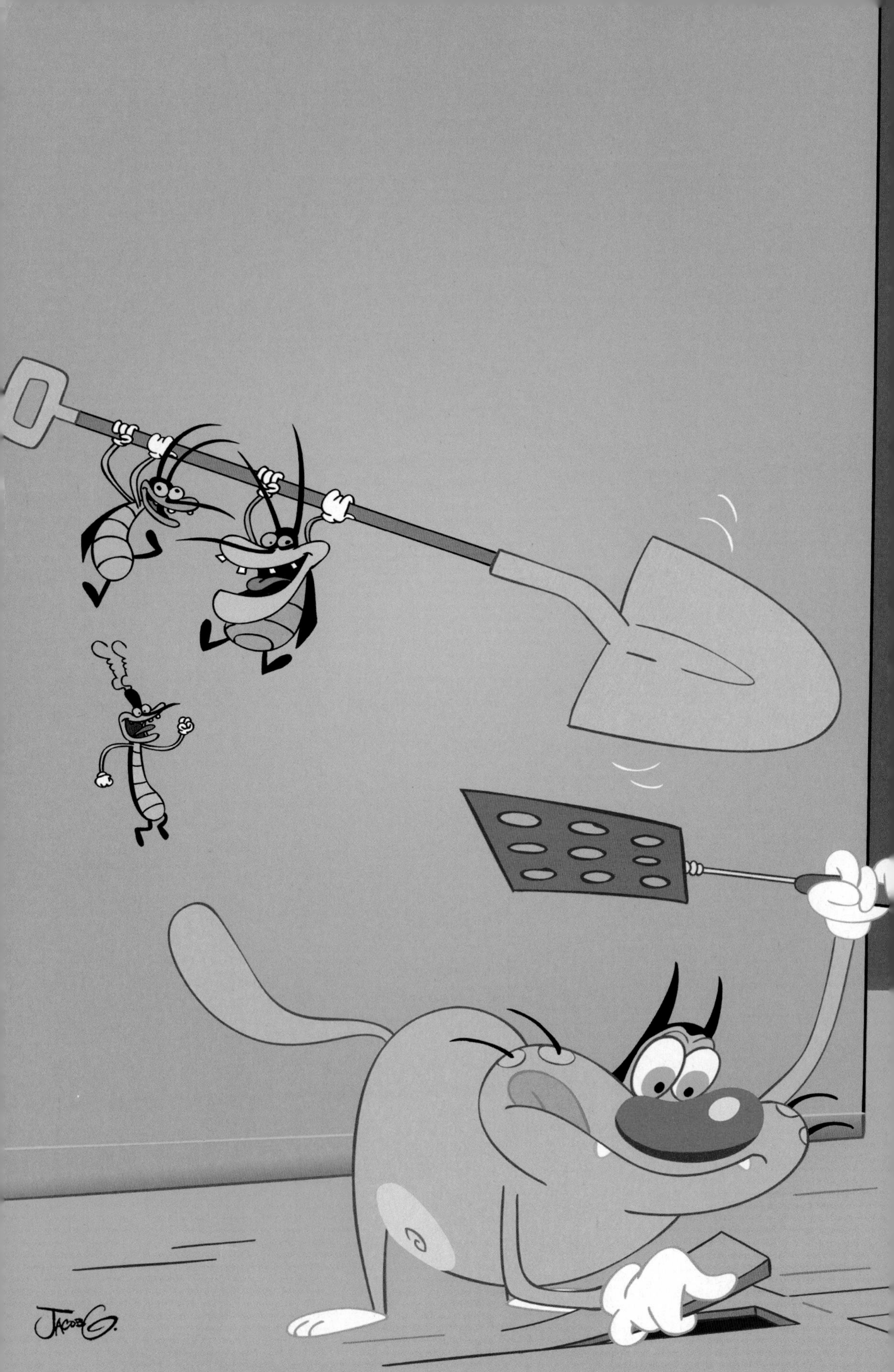
JACOB G.

Cover art by Jacob Greenawalt

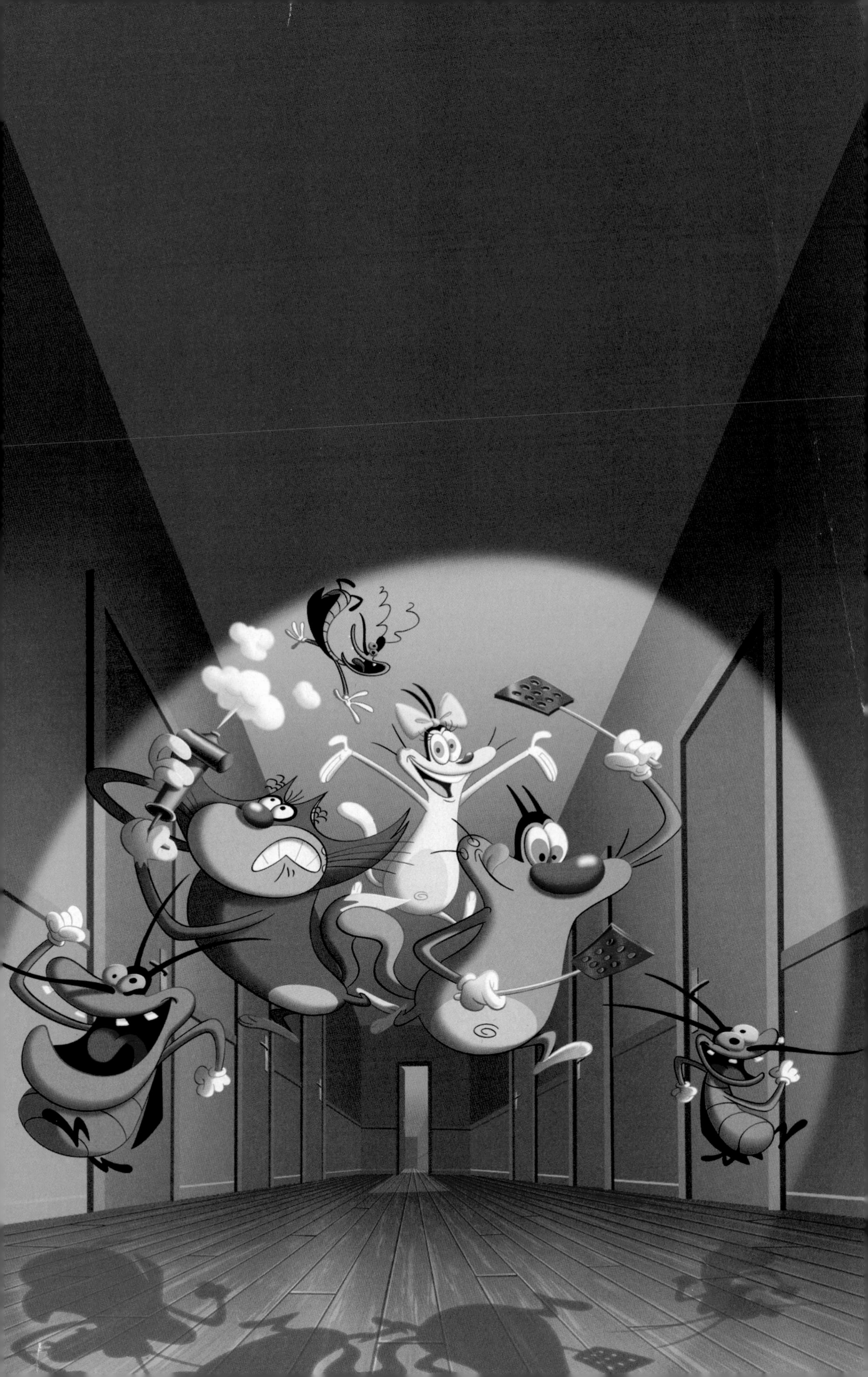

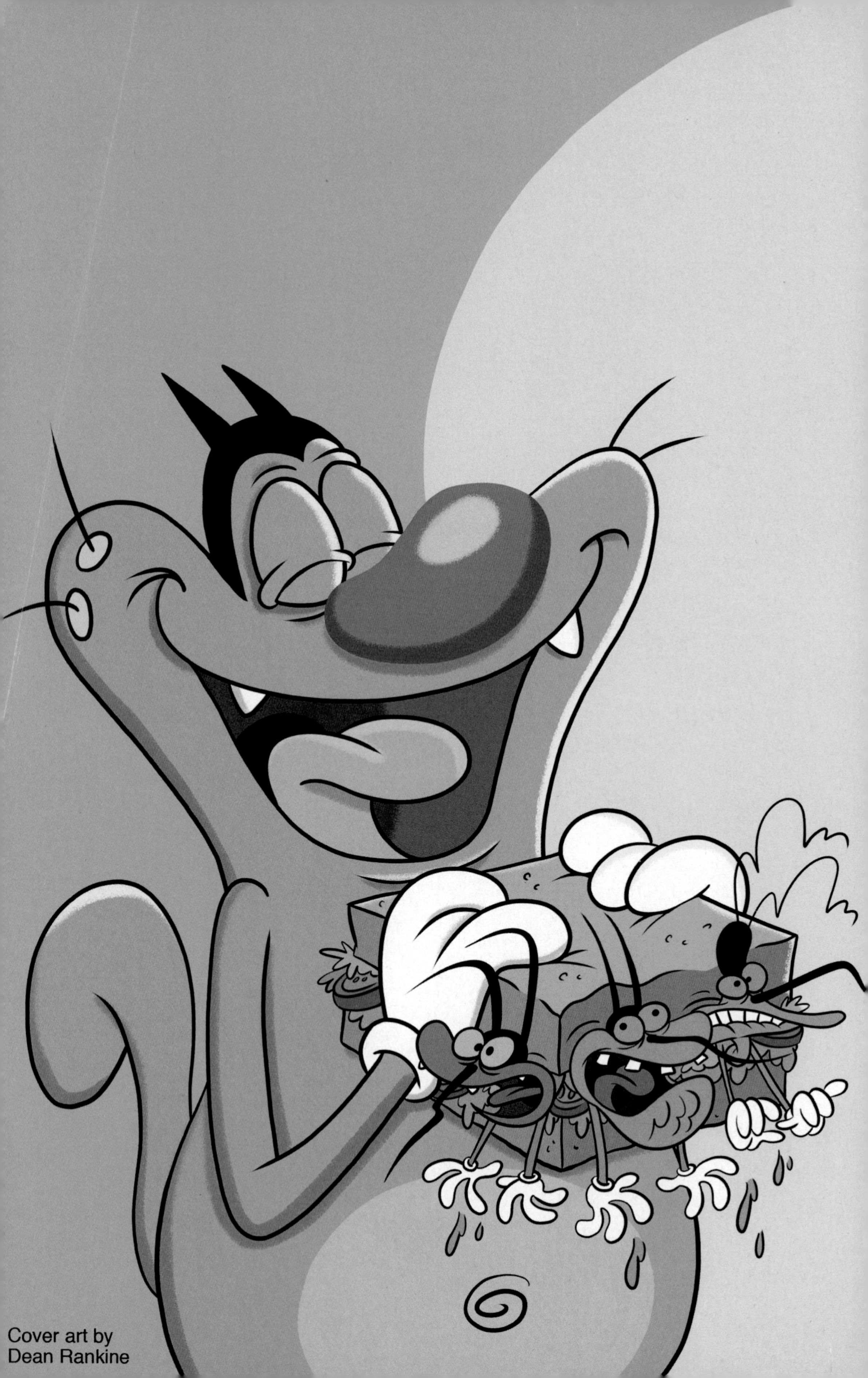

Cover art by
Dean Rankine

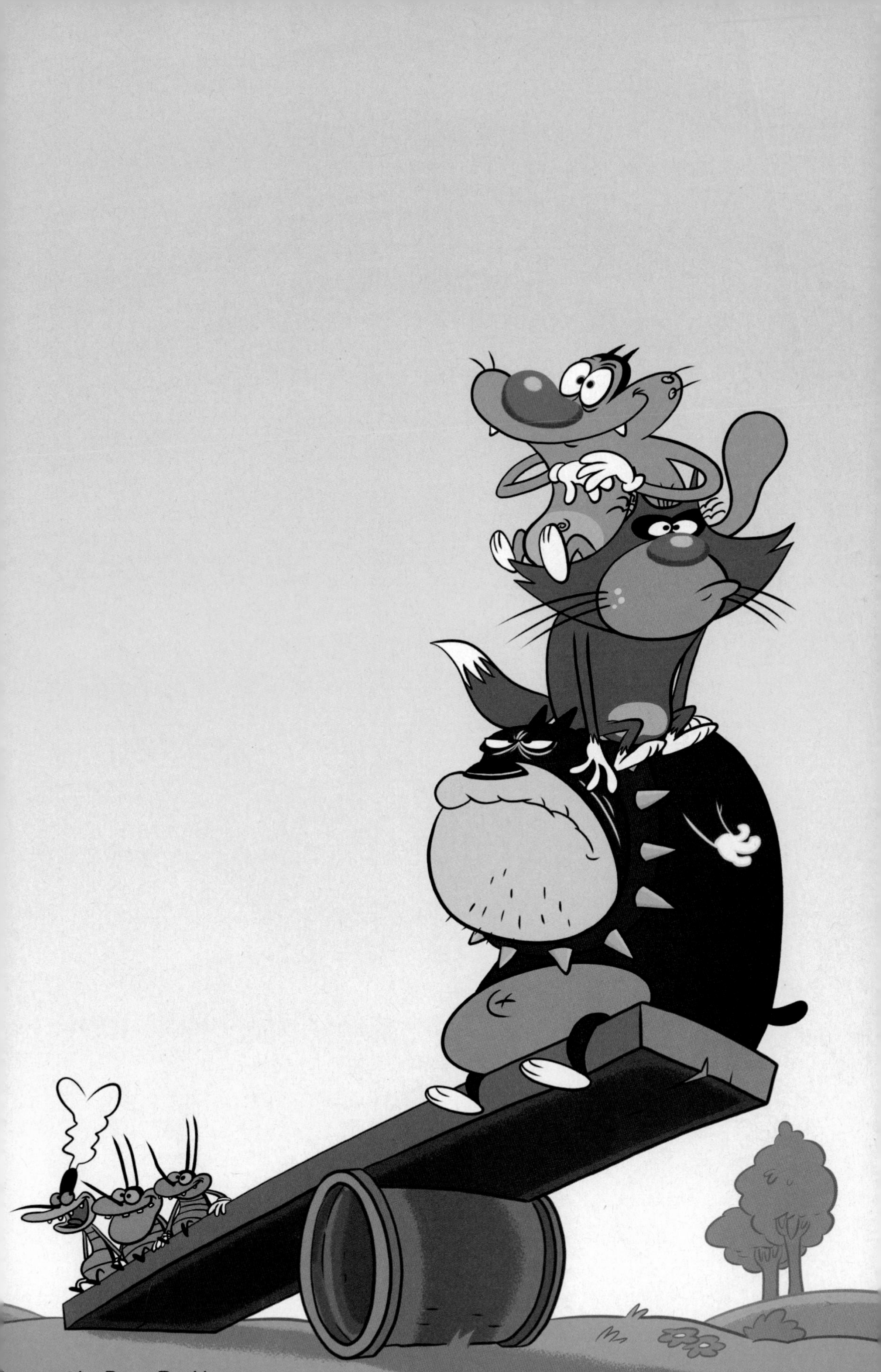

Cover art by Dean Rankine

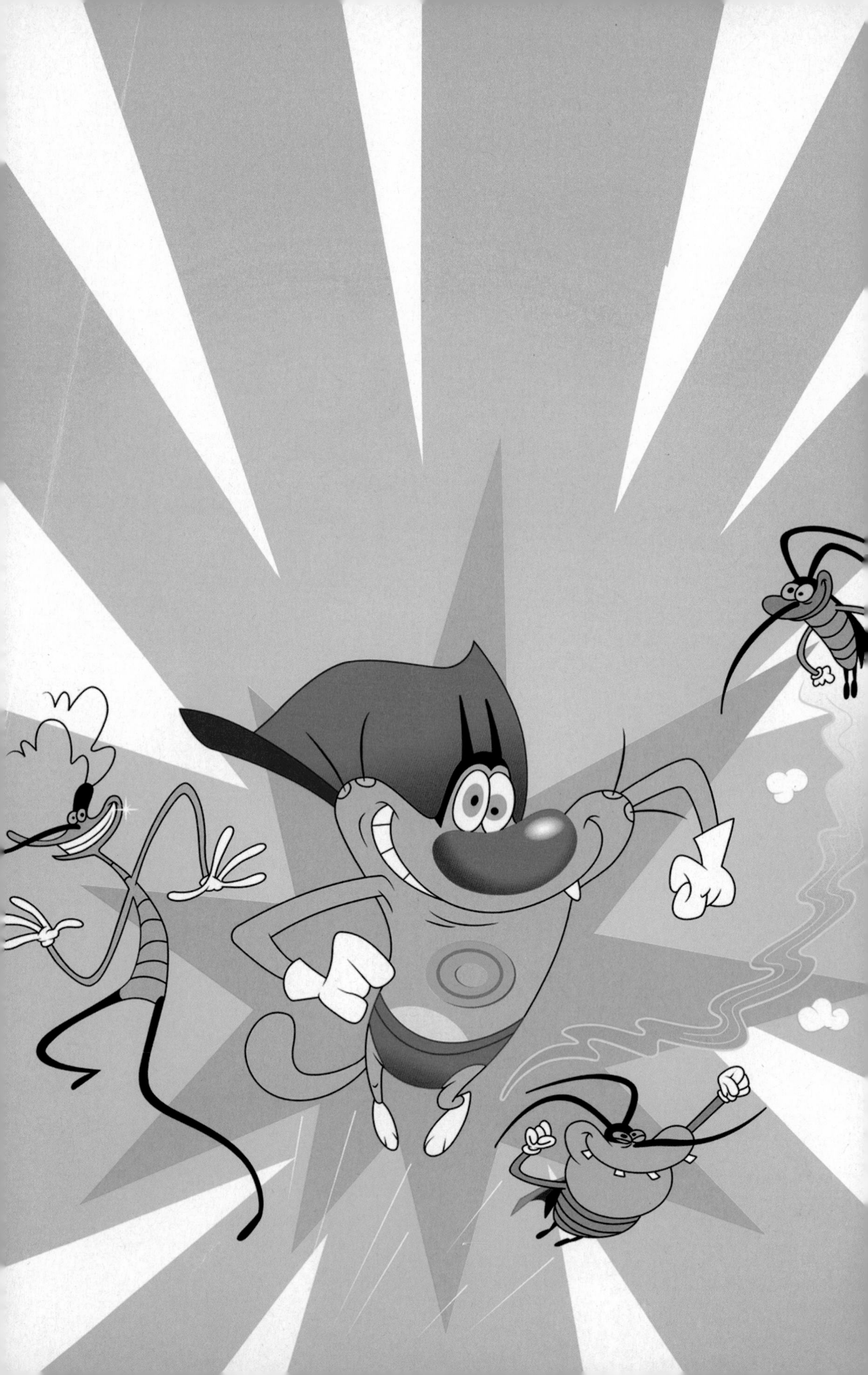

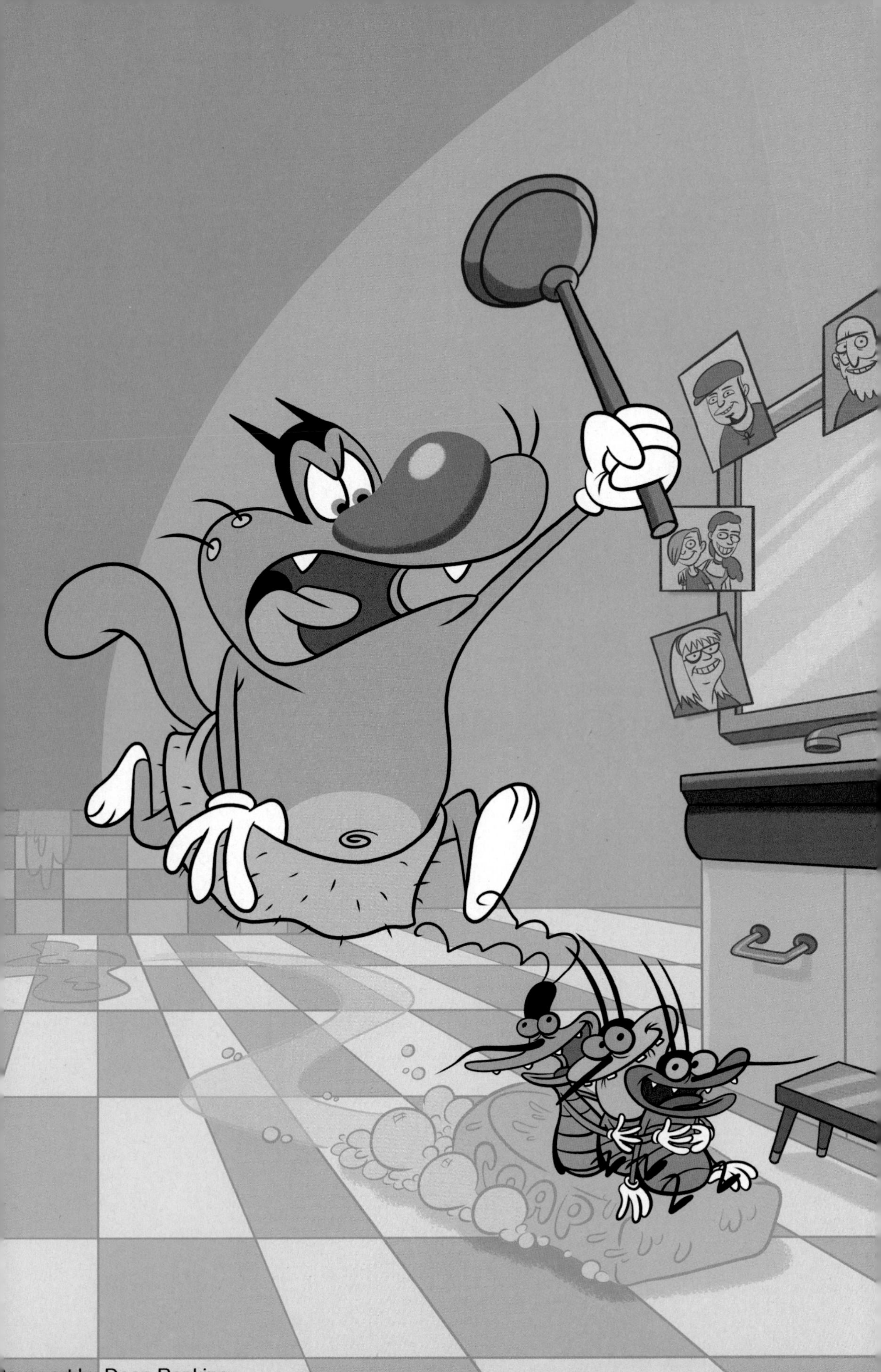
SOAP

Cover art by Dean Rankine

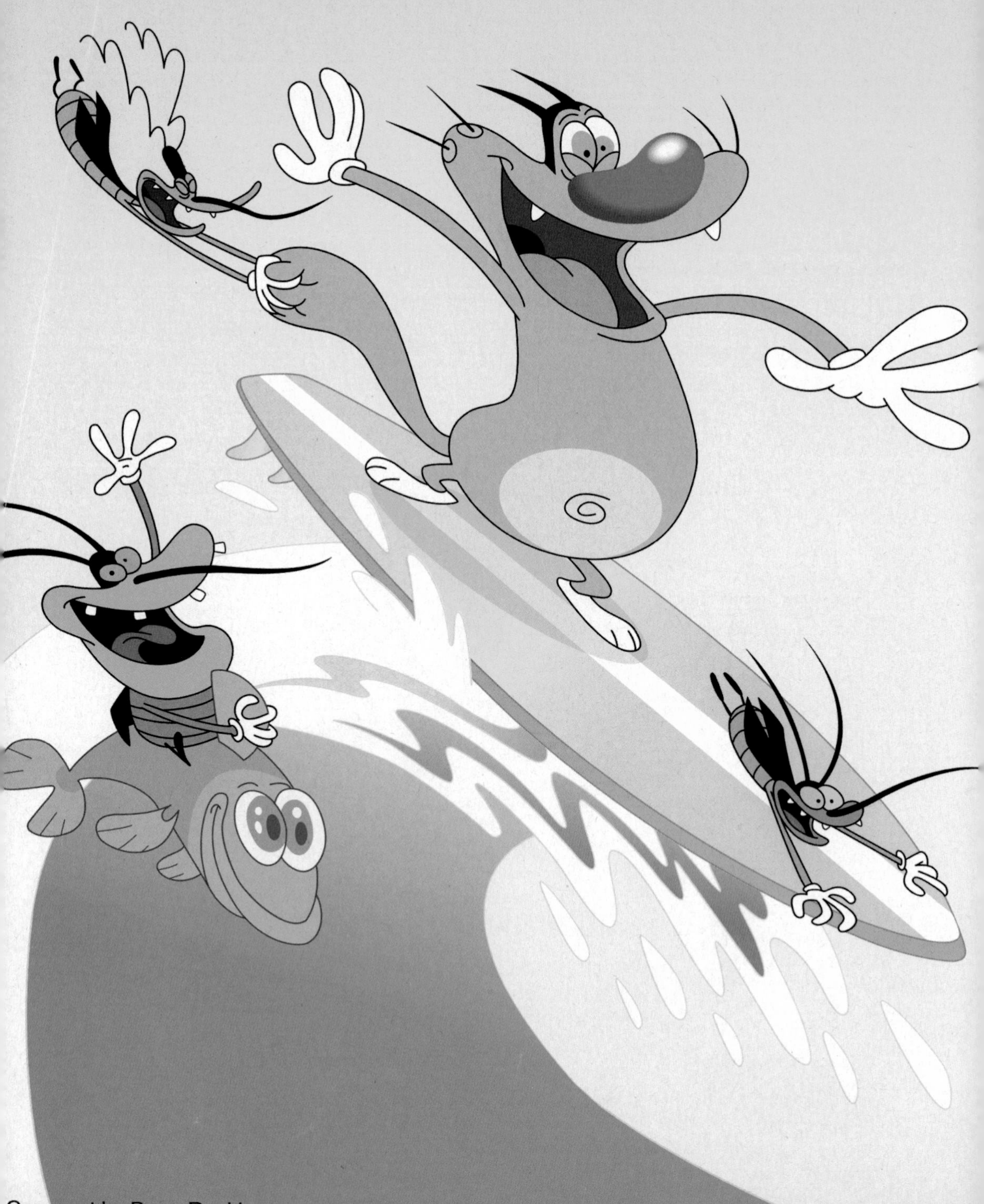

Cover art by Dean Rankine

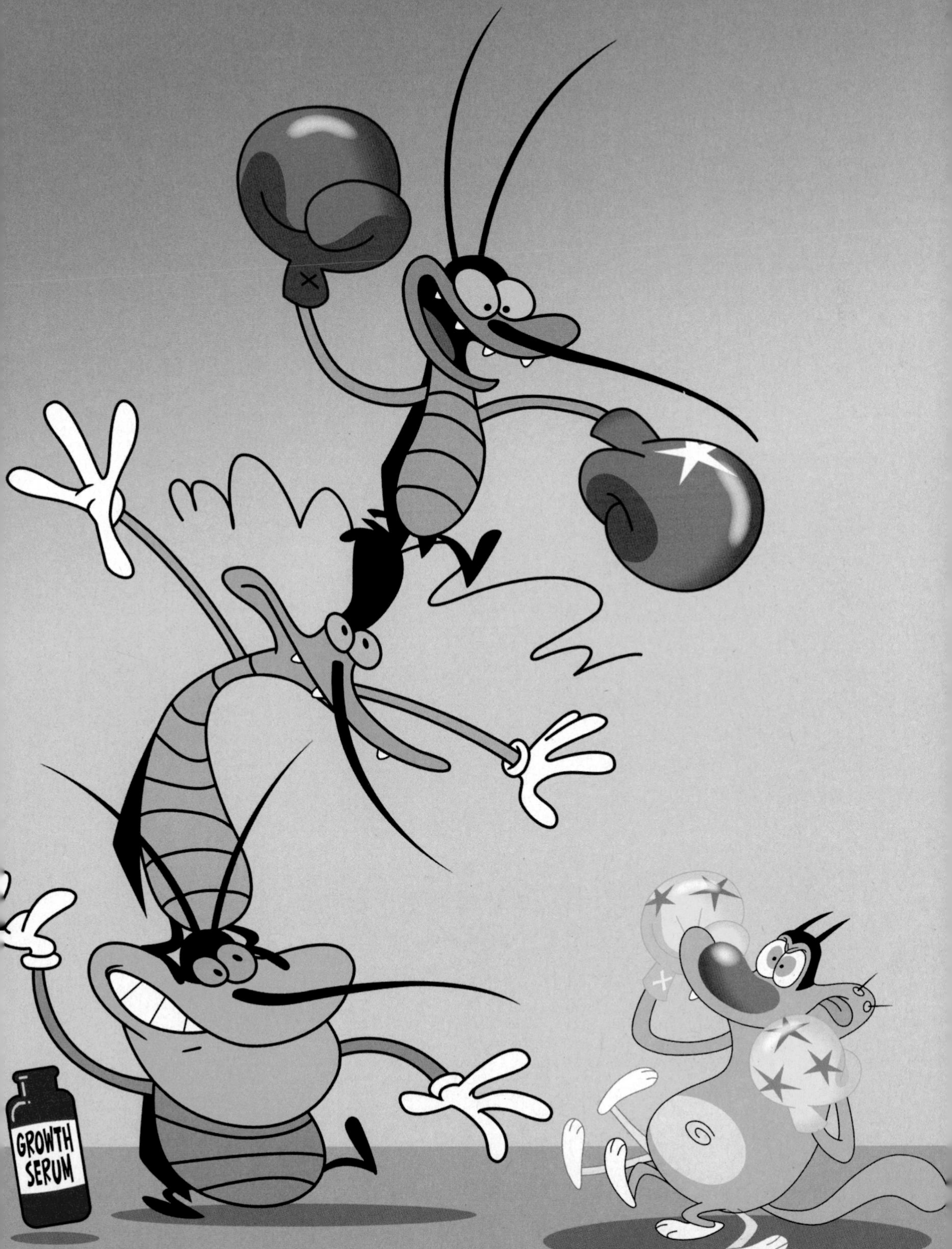
GROWTH SERUM